Love at Leighton Lake

Samantha Hicks

Affinity
Rainbow Publications

2021

Love at Leighton Lake
© 2021 by Samantha Hicks

Affinity E-Book Press NZ LTD.
Canterbury, New Zealand

1st Edition

ISBN:
978-1-99-004923-1
All rights reserved.

Editor: Raven's Eye Editing, CK King
Proof Editor: Alexis Smith
Cover Design: Irish Dragon Designs
Production Design: Affinity Publication Services

Editor: Raven's Eye Editing, CK King
Proof Editor: Alexis Smith
Cover Design: Irish Dragon Designs
Production Design: Affinity Publication Services

Acknowledgments

These past eighteen months have been difficult for every single person on the planet, all fighting the same virus that has killed so many and long-term affected others. I don't think there is anybody Covid hasn't touched in one way or the other. We often turn to the creative arts to bring us joy and entertain us, this has never been truer during these dark times. I hope, in some small way, that my books have helped ease the darkness we are all in, and they have taken your mind off the current crisis, if only for a little while.

Love at Leighton Lake will be my seventh novel with Affinity and was written in the midst of the pandemic. Inspiration came from the short holiday I managed to take with my parents before we were hit with another lockdown. Three of my biggest loves are cabins, water, and Devon. Setting the novel there was a no brainer.

As always, my deepest gratitude goes to the team behind Affinity. They work tirelessly to bring out high quality stories we all enjoy, even during this pandemic. I love working with them and can't see myself ever wanting to find another home for my work. They are an amazing bunch and so too are my fellow Affinity writers, who offer support and encouragement.

I owe my biggest thanks to CK for, again, making my writing look like I know what I'm doing. With every novel we collaborate on, I learn a little more. She has given me invaluable guidance and advice I take with me into each new story.

I couldn't have got through this year without Finley. His doggie kisses and nighttime snuggles makes my heart so full of love for him. I couldn't ask for a better best friend.

DEDICATION

For Hannah

Thank you for putting up with my crazy self and being best buds with Finley. You make our days brighter and fill them with laughter.

TABLE OF CONTENTS

Love at Leighton Lake

Samantha Hicks

CHAPTER ONE

"I don't understand why you're making such a fuss." Tally grimaced, as she tried to settle her leg into a more comfortable position. She shuffled back into the couch and attempted to lift her leg onto the pillow. Danielle frowned and sighed at her daughter, then moved her hand under Tally's calf and helped lift her leg onto the sofa. Tally groaned, as her hip muscle spasmed from the movement. It had been three months since she was attacked, while on duty with the police force, and the pain hadn't lessened any in that time. Tally was sure the doctors were wrong, and she would never get back to full health. She smiled her thanks at Danielle. "It'll only be for a few months."

"I'm not making a fuss. I just don't see why you must move halfway across the country. There will be no one there to help you."

"I've already found a physiotherapist local to the cabin, who is happy to come out and see me. I won't need to drive around or anything."

Danielle sat in the adjacent armchair, her brows pulled down as she glared at Tally. "And what about your personal needs? You haven't been able to shower by yourself since you came out of the hospital. Who's going to do your shopping? What if you get a cramp in the middle of the night? Who will help stretch it out?"

These were all valid points, but the thought of staying in Nottingham was harder to bear than the thought of being alone in Devon. Tally would find a way to manage. It was true she needed help in the shower. Standing for longer than a few minutes at a time was torture. Aside from that, Tally didn't need much looking after. She could make toast when she was hungry and had no problems dressing herself. There was no need for her mother to be so worried. Her health insurance payout would be hitting her bank account any day, so she had the money to rent the cabin for as long as she wanted. Tally would only need to pay for essentials, and that was no different from staying at home. A few weeks living by the lake, surrounded by nature, sounded heavenly. There was no better medicine than fresh air. She couldn't get that cooped up in her tiny one-bedroom flat.

"Is this because of Annabelle?"

Tally's stomach clenched at the mention of her ex. After the attack, Annabelle had been a godsend. She cared for Tally night and day. Tally had hated having to rely on her girlfriend for help, but Annabelle promised it was fine. She loved Tally and would do anything for her. It turned out those were empty words. Within four weeks of Tally coming home, Annabelle packed her stuff and left...while Tally slept. Awakened by her mother an hour later, Tally learned that Annabelle had texted Danielle to say she was sorry and to ask Danielle to check on Tally. She didn't cry, too shocked that Annabelle hadn't even said goodbye. It was Tally's fault. She had been a burden on Annabelle. She promised herself she wouldn't do that again to anyone. Danielle assumed the role of primary carer after Annabelle left, and Tally hated this just as much. Her mother was in her sixties and had retired from work less than a year ago. Tally didn't like it that her mother now had to care for her.

"I haven't even heard from Annabelle since she left. My decision to go has nothing to do with her." *Well, mostly.* The flat they shared for three years had been the perfect starter home, cheap enough so they could save money for the future. They had planned to buy their own house one day, even talked about having children. Tally couldn't believe Annabelle had just walked out on her after everything they had been through.

Tally glanced around the living room, seeing the spaces where Annabelle's things used to be. It was depressing enough looking at the same four walls through months of recovery; it was worse now Annabelle's stuff was gone. Tally needed to get away and clear her head.

"Then what is it?" Danielle asked.

"I just want to get away for a while. Somewhere different than here."

"I could come with you." Danielle shrugged a shoulder. "It's been a while since I caught up with Selma. I'd love to see her place."

Selma Matthews had been Danielle's best friend since their early twenties and was the owner of the cabin Tally would be staying in. Over the years, Selma and Danielle had drifted apart, life getting in the way, Tally supposed. They sent yearly updates through Christmas cards and occasional phone calls, but they hadn't seen each other in way over ten years. Selma was busy running the campsite and raising a family, while Danielle had her own family to bring up and work to do. The campsite was the first place Tally thought of when she decided she needed to get away for a while.

"Mum, you and Dad are supposed to be going on your cruise in a couple of weeks. You've both worked really hard and deserve not to have your plans ruined because of me."

A flash of anger zipped across Danielle's face. "If you think a stupid holiday is more important than my daughter, then you're an idiot. We can take the cruise another time when you're back on your feet."

"I don't want you to. I need to do this on my own, to get back my independence. I don't want to have to rely on you forever."

"It won't be forever. Tallulah, you went through something horrific. No one expects you to just bounce back after something like that. Mentally *or* physically. You need help. I'm your mother. I'm not going to abandon you so I can go sailing for three months with your father."

Tally appreciated those words. It felt good to know her mother would always be on her side, but she needed to do this by herself. She wouldn't feel normal again if she kept depending on Danielle.

"Please, Mum. Please, just let me go."

Danielle silently eyed Tally, her arms folded across her chest. She blew out a breath. "How will you get there? You can't drive."

Tally smiled, glad she had gained her mother's support. "Jimmy said he'd take me."

"You talked to your brother about this before me?"

"I needed to make sure I could get down there before I made the final decision to go."

"I could have dropped you off."

"True, but I also know you wouldn't have left me there on my own."

"You're right, I wouldn't have. So, it's all settled then? You're off to Devon."

"I know you don't like it, but Selma will be there if I get into trouble. She'll be the first to call you if there's a problem."

Danielle stood and approached Tally. She kissed her forehead. "She better do. You're my little girl, and I don't want anything to happen to you, not again." A few tears gathered in the corners of Danielle's eyes. Tally knew she was thinking of the night of the attack.

"I'll be fine. I promise."

"Your father won't like this."

Tally laughed. The shaking of her body brought a stab of pain in her pelvis, where several metal pins held things in place. She tried to hide the grimace, lest Danielle forbid her from leaving. Not that it was up to Danielle, but there were only so many battles Tally could win against her mother.

"Dad worries more than you do. I'm sure you'll be able to talk him around, though."

"If you're still down there when we get back, we'll come down for a visit."

"That would be great."

"I think Caitlyn works there, as well, now. It'll be nice for you to meet up with her again."

"Caitlyn? She's Selma's daughter, isn't she?"

Danielle sat back in the armchair, a wistful smile coming to her lips. "Yes. You two used to play all the time when you were toddlers."

Tally thought hard, casting her mind back thirty years. She vaguely remembered playing with a shy, dark-haired girl. She gazed at Danielle. "I don't really remember her much."

"You were only four the last time you saw her." Danielle sighed, glancing up to the ceiling. "God, I can't believe so many years have passed."

"How come I never saw her when Selma visited? Or when we stayed at the cabin, for that matter."

"Caitlyn spent a lot of time with her dad after Selma and he divorced. Selma came up here on her own. It would have been nice for you and Caitlyn to have stayed friends, but that's life, I suppose. You'll be best friends before you know it."

"We haven't seen each other in thirty years. We were kids. We probably won't even like each other. And don't forget, I'm going there to rest and get better, not to make new friends."

"You can never have too many friends, Tallulah."

Tally didn't agree. She preferred her own space and solitude. The handful of friends she had were enough for her. She'd surprised herself when she asked Annabelle to move in with her. She had thought she was happy seeing her only once a week. She found, though, that she couldn't get enough of Annabelle. The time they spent together was thrilling. Tally wouldn't be making that mistake again. *My heart is my own from now on. I can't count on anyone. Well, except my family.*

Not wanting to upset her mother, she said, "I guess it would be nice to have someone to talk to."

Danielle smiled widely. "Selma is good people, I'm sure her daughter is just as nice. Right. Tell me where I can find a pen and some paper. We need to make a list of everything you need to take with you."

For the next hour, they talked through the things Tally would need for an extended stay down south. Tally's initial excitement at gaining her independence back began to wane. The reality of knowing she would be completely by herself flared a kernel of doubt. She'd have twice-weekly visits from the physio, and the campsite staff would do housekeeping, but everything else would be down to Tally. She wasn't planning on going far, sitting on the deck, and watching the lake would be her entertainment. She knew she could handle that. However, Danielle was right. How would she manage her shower and cooking meals? She could barely sit on the sofa without intense pain. *Guess I'll find out. And who cares if I don't shower for weeks. It's not like I'm planning on seeing anyone. A strip wash would be more than adequate. Let's hope Caitlyn and Selma don't mind me stinking up the place.* She smiled to herself.

†

"How was the water?"

Caitlyn glanced up from her cereal bowl, as her mother approached the table with phone and day planner in hand. She settled in the opposite seat and poured herself a cup of coffee from the carafe and took a sip. The sun had risen an hour ago, but was still low enough in the sky to cast an orange glow over her mother's face. At sixty-two, Selma

Matthews retained a youthful appearance. Hardly any lines marred her face, and the grey just touched her short, dark hair at the temples. Considering Selma worked most of the day out in nature, she didn't look a day over forty-five. Caitlyn hoped she had her mother's good genes. She was coming up to thirty-four in a few weeks. *Some days, I swear Mum has more energy than I do.* "Frigid." Caitlyn spooned in another mouthful of Weetos and chewed for a moment, while her mum laughed.

"I have no idea how you have the guts to get into that lake every morning."

Caitlyn hadn't missed a day in the lake since she arrived back home eight years ago. She had always loved swimming, but the local pool was ten miles away. It was much easier to roll out of bed, stride across the dock, and dive right into the waters of Leighton Lake. The first time had nearly given her a heart attack. All the breath left her and, for a moment, she panicked she was drowning. She managed to calm herself and started a front crawl over the still, dark water. The buzz she got from the cold water was an exhilarating start to each day.

"I don't understand how you haven't done it once since you bought the place."

"I fell in once, while trying to tie up the dinghy. It's not an experience I want to repeat."

Caitlyn smiled. "You're missing out."

"I'm surprised you haven't caught anything yet. God only knows what kind of bacteria is floating about in there. Including fish poop."

"I've got a strong immune system." Caitlyn stood and took her now-empty bowl to the sink. "Anytime you want to give it go, just let me know."

"Over my dead body."

Caitlyn laughed at the horrified look on her mother's face.

Selma had owned Leighton Lake for about twenty-five years, along with the seven cabins nestled amongst the woods in a ring around the lake. The peaceful place was full of wildlife and greenery. In the busiest summer months, families would come from the cities to experience life outside of the smog-filled towns. Most guests acclimatised fine, but the different pace of life was a major culture shock for some. Caitlyn recalled having to swim out to the centre of the lake to rescue a screaming woman whose husband had flipped the Jet Ski. Despite the woman wearing a lifejacket, she flailed about gasping for breath. Once Caitlyn pulled her in, the woman made her husband pack up the car. They were gone within the hour. Suffice to say, the great outdoors wasn't for everyone.

"So, what's on the agenda today?" Caitlyn asked, retaking her seat.

Selma opened the day planner in front of her and scanned the pages. They had gotten into this routine quickly since Caitlyn's arrival. Selma ran the place with precision. Nothing happened on the lake she didn't know about. She had a small staff of five people, including Caitlyn, that saw to the upkeep of the grounds and cabins.

"Fredrick will be fixing the broken boards on the dock and checking on the leak in Cabin Four. Steve is going to do a perimeter check for me." Selma glanced up. "Apparently, one of the Johnsons' cows was spotted roaming the woods by the guests in Two. I'm not sure if it's true or not, so Steve will need to do a full circuit around the property." It wasn't the first time one of the animals from the neighbouring farm had found its way onto the property, and it probably wouldn't be the last. "We have new arrivals coming after lunch. I need you to change the sheets and put fresh towels in the bathrooms. Also, can you make a list of essentials we need for their pantries and fridges?"

"Of course. I'll make a run out to the shop about eleven." The cabins were self-catering, but her mother always liked to have a few things in stock to help the new arrivals in case they forgot anything. It was a nice touch and one that helped boost Leighton Lake's reviews on TripAdvisor.

"Great. Oh, for Cabin Seven, can you double the supplies? Tallulah will be staying in that one, and she won't be able to get around much. I don't want her struggling while she's here."

Caitlyn stared at her mother, her brain desperately trying to work out who the hell Tallulah was. *Why would an old lady be staying here? With a name like Tallulah, she must be nearly ninety.*

"Why are you looking at me funny?"

"Tallulah?"

"Yes, Tallulah. Danielle's daughter."

"Danielle?" If Tallulah is ninety, her mother must be one hundred and twenty. What on earth?

"Do you ever listen to me?" Her mum blew out a breath, shaking her head. "Dee has been my friend for over forty years."

"Oh, Dee." Now she remembered. "Sorry. You never call her Danielle. I didn't know who you meant."

"Sometimes, I swear you listen less than your father ever did."

Caitlyn laughed, knowing it was probably true. His listening skills were one of the reasons Selma divorced him.

She had tried to tell him how unhappy she was in the marriage, but he never listened. In the end, Selma had enough and left him, taking Caitlyn and her brother with her. There wasn't much Caitlyn remembered from her childhood, but the long car rides to and from her dads were forever etched on her memory.

"Anyway," Selma continued. "Tallulah was injured while at work, and she's coming here to recharge her batteries and get better."

"Who names their child Tallulah?"

"It was Dee's grandmother's name." Selma frowned. "Focus, Cait."

"Sorry." Caitlyn blushed. Her mind would often wander from one thing to the next. Her focus had improved over the years, but she still had to concentrate hard on the here and now. *I wonder if I'll ever be normal again.*

"Dee emailed me last night. She didn't go into details of what happened, but she wants us to keep an eye on Tallulah."

Caitlyn grinned and suffered her mum's narrowed her eyes. "I'm sorry. But Tallulah is a very funny name."

"You should count your blessings. I was going to call you Gertrude, after my granny."

Caitlyn shivered at the horror that name would have been.

"She goes by Tally. Do you think you can handle saying that without giggling like a schoolchild?"

"I'll try."

"You'd better. Dee said what happened was horrific. Tallulah doesn't need to come here and have you make fun of her."

"Okay, okay. Jeez, I'm not a monster." She paused for a moment, her mind drifting again. "I wonder if she's disfigured."

"Caitlyn Marie Matthews! What a dreadful thing to say. I raised you better than that."

Caitlyn lowered her head in shame. Her mum was right; it was a mean thing to say. Sometimes Caitlyn couldn't stop herself from being inappropriate. She was trying to devoid herself of the trait, but sometimes her brain forgot to censor itself. "I'm sorry."

"So you should be. Anyway, we need to make her comfortable. Anything she needs, we will aim to provide. She's my best friend's daughter. I won't have her hurting while she's here."

"How come I've never met her?"

"You have. Back when I lived with your father, we would all get together and have playdates. You used to love chasing around with Tallulah."

"How old was I?"

Selma looked skyward, rubbing her chin with her hand. "Probably about three or four. Tally is the same age as you. It was quite the experience to be pregnant at the same time as my best friend. There are only about four months between you."

Caitlyn searched her brain for any kind of memory. There was nothing. "I don't remember her."

Selma smiled sadly at Caitlyn. She reached across and squeezed Caitlyn's arm. "That's not surprising. It was a long time ago. I'll dig out the photo albums, I'm sure there will be some pictures in there of the two of you."

Caitlyn nodded, then withdrew her arm. She stood from the chair and went to the kitchen window. She gazed across the grass, through the trees, and to the lake that lay beyond. The sun was fully in the sky now, the rays bouncing off the water, making the surface look like glass. She heaved a big breath and let it go. She was aware of her mother's gaze on her. "I guess those memories are gone for good now, aren't they?"

"Caitlyn, you know what the doctor told you. We just have to wait and see."

Caitlyn turned her back on the beautiful visage and faced her mother. She wanted to be angry, to scream that it wasn't fair, but one look into that caring gaze made the feelings go away. "I guess it's not all bad. Who wants to remember their mother gave them a home perm that embarrassed them in school."

Selma laughed, the sadness in her eyes slipping away. "Don't forget, I still have the pictures."

Caitlyn was glad of the multitude of photos Selma had taken of her and her brother growing up. Without them, Caitlyn would swear she never belonged to this family. After the accident, Caitlyn couldn't remember a thing, including her name. In the fourteen years since, Caitlyn had recovered partial memories from the first nineteen years of her life. They would come at random times. Sometimes a smell or an image would trigger the memory. In the beginning, the memories came quickly, but she hadn't had a new one in years. A massive chunk of her life was still missing. She needed to make peace with that.

"I'm going to go do the linens and towels. If there is anything else you need me to do before I go to the shop, let me know. I'll have my phone." Caitlyn strode from the room. The buzz from her swim had dwindled. She never gave her memory loss much thought these days. She was so busy working at the lake that she didn't have time for mourning memories she couldn't recall. She found it best to get on with her life. Once she came out of the hospital, she set about gaining as many new memories as possible. Her mother hadn't been pleased that Caitlyn wanted to travel the globe, but Caitlyn wouldn't be swayed. She wanted to see as much of the world as she could. Five years later, she'd had enough. All she wanted was to go home and reconnect with her mother. Being there settled her restless mind. The beauty of the lake suffused her with peace. She never wanted to be anywhere else.

As she loaded up the golf cart with sheets and towels, her thoughts drifted. *Tallulah.* Caitlyn chuckled, trying to imagine what she would look like. *Probably an airheaded bimbo.* She chided herself. It wasn't nice to be making assumptions about one's name. *But still, Tallulah! I wonder what happened to her. Mum would probably kill me if I asked her outright.*

She got into the cart and headed up the gravel track toward the line of cabins. Her gaze drifted to the lake that lay to the left of her. The urge to go swimming was strong. *Maybe once I'm back from the shop I can go for another dip.*

14

CHAPTER TWO

"How are you doing back there?"

Tally caught her brother's gaze in the rearview mirror. Eyes the same emerald shade as her own looked at her with sympathy. "It's a lot better stretched out in the back than keeping my leg bent in the front." It was better, but not by a lot. They had been in the car for nearly three hours. Aside from a stop at the services to refuel, Tally hadn't been able to move about. The jostling of the truck didn't help matters. She had been due to take her latest dose of pain meds an hour ago. The problem was they made her sleepy. She wanted to wait until she was settled in the cabin, so she could lie down and rest for as long as possible. "How much longer, do you think?"

"A couple more miles. It won't be long." Jimmy stayed quiet for a minute, navigating the back roads toward Leighton Lake. "I don't want to sound like Mum, but are you sure this is a good idea? You look like you're in a lot of pain."

Tally sighed. The constant questioning of her judgment was wearing thin. In the two weeks since she told Danielle her plan, Tally had received no less than thirty calls from all her family asking the same thing over and over again. She tried not to let it get to her, but it was a struggle. "Jimbo, I'm fine. It's just not being able to move back here is cramping my hip. Once I get out of the truck and stretch out in bed, I'll be fine."

"Well, if you're sure."

"I'm positive."

"And you're sure you don't want me to stay the night? I'm sure Alice won't mind if I stay with you."

"Thanks for the offer, but you know Alice. She'll ring Mum, and before you know it, Mum will be down here insisting on taking me home."

"Yeah, my wife isn't one for keeping quiet."

Tally leaned forward and squeezed Jimmy's shoulder. "I appreciate all of your concerns, but honestly, I'll be fine."

Jimmy nodded. He slowed and turned down a narrow track. Tally glanced at the thick trees, as the truck rolled by. She smiled. It had been a long time, but she still recognised the trail leading to the lake. Already her heart felt lighter, the pain in her hip subsiding. After a few more minutes of driving, the sign for Leighton Lake Cabins came into view. The wood was cracked and scarred, the paint peeling off in places, but it didn't look old. It was almost like the sign had been designed to have a rustic style in keeping with the cabins.

From what Tally remembered, the cabins were old-fashioned and simple, with cast iron range cookers, tea kettles you could warm over the fireplace or cooker and washing machines you cranked by hand. The last time Tally stayed, she'd found an electric kettle and toaster in the cabin for guests who couldn't figure out how to use the fireplace. The design was made to feel like a true cabin experience, only you didn't have to go out and hunt for your food. There was a small fishing lake on the other side of the woods and plenty of walking trails. The only modern conveniences were the Jet Skis and paddle boats. Danielle had told Tally that Selma only added them because some of the guests complained they were bored. Tally didn't understand their reasoning. Why would you book a holiday in a secluded cabin if you weren't looking forward to the peace and quiet?

Lost in her thoughts, Tally didn't notice Jimmy had come to a stop outside the main house. Not much had changed with that building either. Net curtains flapped out the open windows. Logs were stacked by the door, and an old rocking chair faced the midday sun looking out toward the lake behind the trees. Tally's smile grew wider. She couldn't believe it had been twelve years since she last visited. She reached for the door handle and swivelled her body to lower her legs to the ground.

"Wait!" Jimmy rushed from the driver's side and pushed against her door, preventing her from opening it. "You need your crutches."

In her excitement to breathe in the fresh, winter air, she had forgotten about her leg.

17

Jimmy glared at her. "Give me a minute." He went to the bed of the truck and retrieved her crutches. He opened her door and held them out to her.

"Thanks." She threaded her arms through the wrist holes and grasped the handles. Taking a breath, she gingerly climbed from the back seat. Jimmy helped steady her. The blood rushed down her leg, causing it to throb. Tally pressed her lips together and screwed her eyes shut, fearing she would pass out from the pain. After a moment, her pulse settled and she opened her eyes. She scanned the area. Bright sunshine warmed her skin, despite the chill from the wind. *Yeah, I'm going to love staying here.*

"Go on in. I'll get your bags."

"Thanks. And thanks for getting me here in one piece. I owe you one."

"Anything for my big sister."

Tally swung the crutches forward, followed by her leg. Although she could stand unaided, and walk a few steps, being cooped up in the truck for all that time made the short distance to the door seem impossible. She didn't relish the thought of falling flat on her face. She had done that plenty of times in the past few months. It wasn't a pleasant experience. She shouldered opened the door and stepped inside. This place was also the same as she remembered. A large living room shot off to her left, the kitchen to the right. In front of her was a large oak desk beneath a sign that hung from the beams and read *Reception*. The scents of wood and bacon permeated the air. Tally instantly felt at home. She went over to the desk and dinged the little bell that sat next to a large, desk calendar. A tall, robust woman rounded the corner from the kitchen. She was the same height as Tally's five eight, but a good thirty pounds heavier. Her blue eyes contrasted with her dark, greying hair. It may have been over a decade since Tally saw her last, but she would recognise Selma anywhere.

"Tallulah! You made it."

"It's good to see you, Selma."

Selma tossed the tea towel she was holding onto the desk and wrapped her strong arms around Tally. Tally clumsily held on, the crutches dangling from her arms.

"Let me look at you." Selma held her at arm's length, lips smiling, eyes shining. "You look just like your mother."

"And you haven't changed one bit."

Selma's cheeks heated. "Where's Jimmy?"

"Here I am."

Tally turned her head to see Jimmy standing by the door, suitcases in his hands. He didn't have time to drop them before Selma hugged him much the same way she had Tally.

"My, my," Selma said. "You've grown into such a handsome man. Still married?"

"Yes."

"That's a shame. A young guy like you living here would have all the cabins filled in no time. You could be the repair person. I'd for sure get repeat business."

Jimmy's cheeks flamed. "I don't think my wife would be too happy if I started doing DIY for the single ladies."

"Probably not." Selma chuckled. She turned back to Tally, her features becoming serious. "Dee didn't go into details, but I know you were hurt pretty badly. How are you doing?"

Tally shrugged, then smiled. Her leg was on fire, but she'd had enough of people fussing over her. She wanted normality back, so she lied. "Much better. Won't be long before I'm on the beat again."

"You'll be going back to the force?"

"I guess. I'm not qualified for anything else." She wasn't looking forward to that day. She still had nightmares about the attack. The thought of putting her uniform back on broke her out in a cold sweat.

"Well, let's get you checked in and shown to your cabin. I imagine you can't wait to get off your feet."

"You read my mind."

Selma went around the desk and booted up the computer. "I've given you Cabin Seven. It's the most secluded, but it has the best view of the lake. Fredrick has got an old golf cart fixed up. You can keep that for your own use. You don't want to have to be struggling down the track."

"I don't need special treatment."

Selma's eyes widened, a look of hurt flashing across her face. "This isn't special treatment, it's customer service. We did the same a while back for a gentleman who twisted his ankle. We pride ourselves on doing everything we can for our guests."

"Okay. I'm sorry."

"It's fine." Selma waved her hand. "Don't worry about it. Linens and towels are changed once a week. If you need it done more often, just let me know. Cabin Seven's cleaning day is Tuesday mornings. Will that be okay?"

"Perfect."

"The pantry and fridge have been stocked with some essentials for you. I know you've brought your own food, but it's there if you want it. I know you won't be travelling. We go to the shop all the time. Anything you need, just give me a holler and I'll add it to the list." Selma handed Tally two keys. "This one is for the door, that one is for the cart. Please, no joyriding."

Tally laughed, as she stuffed the keys into her pocket. "I'm a little old for joyriding."

"Nonsense. You're never too old to go for a good spin." Selma waggled her eyebrows.

Jimmy coughed. "That's my cue to leave."

"Already?" Selma asked. "You've just got here."

"I know, but it's a long drive back. It's been good to see you, Selma. I'll bring the wife and kids down for a holiday as soon as I can."

"It's lovely to see you, too. Say hi to your mum for me."

"Will do."

Jimmy hugged Selma, then Tally. "Look after yourself, Sis. Any problems, just call."

"Thanks, I will. Drive safely."

Once Jimmy left, Tally turned back to Selma. "Do you think we can go to the cabin now? I need to lie down." She was surprised she was still standing. Her arms were shaking with the effort of keeping herself upright.

"Of course, come on. My cart is around the back. Leave the bags, and I'll have Fredrick bring them to you in a minute."

Together, they headed through the house. Selma pulled open the back door for Tally to go through first. At Tally's first step over the threshold, something hard slammed into her. Not having the strength to keep herself upright, she flew back and landed on the hard floorboards. An atomic mushroom of pain overtook her body. She couldn't stop the tears that flooded her eyes. She didn't know what hurt more, ribs, leg, or pride.

"Oh my God. I am so sorry."

"Caitlyn, you idiot."

"I'm so, so sorry."

Tally felt hands on her. She opened her eyes, her vision swimming. Selma was to the left of her, her terror apparent. Tally looked to the right. A face she had never seen before hovered inches from her own. She couldn't focus on the features, but knew it was a woman.

"Help me get her up," Selma said.

"No! Wait." Tally needed a minute to orientate herself before attempting to stand.

"You are so clumsy," Selma said.

"I'm sorry, Mum. I didn't see her."

"What would Dee say if she found out we broke her daughter within the first hour?"

Tally took a few deep breaths, the pain subsiding. She glanced at Selma. "This does not leave this room. I can't have her worrying about me."

"That's a mother's job."

"Maybe so, but she's done enough worrying for now. Help me up." Selma hooked her arms under Tally's armpits and lifted. Tally held her breath, but her hip screamed in pain.

"Get her crutches," Selma said to the woman, Caitlyn.

Caitlyn bent and picked them up. She handed them over without looking at Tally. Her hair obscured her face, so Tally couldn't see her properly. "Thank you."

"I have to go." Caitlyn rushed past. The sound of feet pounding up the stairs vibrated through the house.

"That's my daughter, the idiot."

"She's not an idiot. It was an accident."

"She has those a lot." Selma sounded frustrated but didn't comment further. "Are you okay?"

Tally nodded. "I'm fine. Just embarrassed."

"Let's get you settled."

Tally got into the cart, and soon, Selma was driving them to the cabin. She helped Tally up the steps and in through the door. Tally didn't stop to look around inside. She asked where the bedroom was and promptly lay down.

"Thank you, Selma."

"Are you sure you're okay?"

"Yes, just tired from the drive. Do you think you can hold off on getting my bags? I just need to take a nap for a bit."

"Of course. There's a phone in the living room. Press One, and it'll connect to the main house. Just call me when you're ready, and we'll bring them to you."

"Thank you."

Tally heard the front door click shut. She fished her pain meds from her trouser pocket and dry-swallowed two. Eventually, the pain ebbed away and her eyes drifted shut. Images of black hair danced behind her eyelids. *I wish I had gotten a look at her face. She sounded so upset. Caitlyn. What a wonderful name.*

†

"What were you thinking?"

"I'm sorry, Mum. I honestly didn't see her there. I didn't expect anyone to be behind the door." Caitlyn kept her head down, as her mother paced in front of her with palpable anger. *It's not my fault that woman came swinging over the threshold.* Caitlyn chanced a glance at her mum. "Is she okay?"

"She said she was, but it was easy to see how much pain she was in." Selma stopped her pacing and knelt by Caitlyn. "Cait, you've got to be more careful." She placed her hand on Caitlyn's knee. "I know you have an abundance of energy, but you need to focus on what you're doing."

"It's not my fault." Caitlyn hated sounding like a child, but it wasn't like she wanted to be this way. Her brain was all messed up after the accident. Her synapses fired much quicker now, and it was harder to concentrate on one thing. But walking into Tally had nothing to do with her funky brain chemistry. It had been a genuine mishap. "You make it sound like I purposefully pushed her over. It was an accident."

Selma sighed and settled next to Caitlyn on the mattress. "I'm sorry, sweetheart. I don't mean to get frustrated with you. It's been a hard struggle for us all. I just don't want you hurting yourself or anyone else."

Caitlyn had the urge to cry. That was something else she couldn't control. The stupidest thing could bring on the tears. She remembered crying once when a squirrel she had been watching dropped a nut and another squirrel took it. "I'm not that bad, Mum. Sometimes you make me feel like I'm a kid who misbehaves. I'm well into my thirties. I've travelled the globe. I've managed quite well over the years. I don't need you constantly fussing over me."

Selma stayed quiet for a moment. "You're right. You're a grown woman, capable of looking after yourself. I just worry about you."

"I guess that's something I have in common with Dee's daughter. You both worry about us."

"Yes. Why were you rushing in here anyway?"

"I finished stocking the cabins as you asked. I was going to get in a quick swim before I started on the paperwork."

Selma shook her head. "You and that bloody lake. Go on then, just be—"

"I know, careful."

"Yes."

Selma left and Caitlyn changed into her swimming gear. Her need for the buzz of the frigid water was stronger than ever. As the day wore on, her thoughts would become more scattered, more restless. The freezing lake somehow helped slow her thoughts down enough that she could concentrate on the tasks she needed to complete. After her talk with her mother this morning, and thinking of the childhood she had lost, her thoughts had jumbled more than usual. It was that need to silence them that had propelled her into the house and straight into the solid body of Tallulah Roberts. *She's definitely not an airhead.* Tally's dark blonde hair was cut short around the ears and framed a square, strong jawline. Caitlyn had only glimpsed a view of mesmerising eyes. She had never seen that shade of green before. *Almost luminous, like a cat.* Tally was taller than Caitlyn by three or four inches. Running into her had felt like hitting a brick wall. Caitlyn had no doubt; if Tally didn't have the crutches, it would have been herself flat on her ass and not Tally. *She smelled really good, too.* Caitlyn shook her head. She had no business ruminating on her mother's best friend's daughter, no matter how hot she was. *I doubt she'll even want to speak to me again, not after I ploughed her over.*

Caitlyn grabbed her goggles and a spare towel, then trotted down to the lake's edge. She dumped the towel onto the dock and dived headfirst into the water. Like always, the first touch of cold water against her skin knocked the breath from her. She was used to this feeling now. She surfaced, took a gulp of air, and began her crawl across the lake. All the jumbled and rambling thoughts left her, as she concentrated on her stroke and breath.

One, two, three, breathe.

One, two, three, breathe.

She found her rhythm and soon glided along the water with ease. Her normal route was the whole perimeter of the lake, taking about ninety minutes. She would swim close to the shoreline, following adjacent to the track that linked the cabins, then loop around back to the dock. It was the safest direction, as she never knew if guests were out on the water. Being close to the shore would hopefully allow people to see her out there, especially with her bright-yellow swim cap. Now, she wasn't thinking about safety. She just wanted to swim. The deeper the water, the harder the challenge. She was frustrated with her mother and herself. She needed to deaden her thoughts as much as she could. Tiring herself out would be the only way to do it. Caitlyn lifted her head and scanned the area. Not seeing anyone out on the water, she ducked back down and aimed her body for the centre of the lake.

CHAPTER THREE

Tally's eyes sprung open. The cramp in her toe had jolted her awake. Her jaw clamped shut, as she struggled to bend her toes. After a moment, the spasm released her muscles, and the pain dissipated. She blinked and took a breath, then glanced around the small room. She hadn't taken the time to notice the details when she arrived, but now allowed her gaze to travel the room. This cabin was like how she remembered her last stay at Leighton Lake. An oak dresser and wardrobe took up one wall. A tight-knit, brightly coloured rug covered the floorboards. The sheets she was under were soft and smelled like the forest. Tally wasn't sure if it was because they were dried outside or if the softener Selma used gave them their scent. She didn't care which, the smell was comforting either way.

She sat up and swung her legs over the edge of the bed. She wasn't sure how long she had slept, but her bladder needed emptying. Tally eyed the crutches that were leaning up against the wall next to the bed and window. She didn't want to keep relying on them. The longer she used them, the longer it would take to fully heal. She also wasn't stupid. Despite being able to walk a few steps without aide, she didn't want to be overconfident and end up causing more damage. *I should be okay with just the one.* She reached out and grabbed one, then hoisted herself to her feet. A slight throb radiated around her pelvis, but no sharp pain. Taking it slowly, she headed out into the main room. The furniture in the living room was styled the same as the bedroom. A sideboard and blanket box sat on either side of the front door. The couch and armchair were made of cracked leather and brass studs. The fireplace was huge and certainly the main feature of the room. Tally turned left into the kitchen, then through to the bathroom.

After taking care of her needs, she went back into the lounge and to the large window that overlooked the lake. Selma had picked the best cabin for Tally. Set only twenty feet from the water's edge, she had a clear view of the lake and the trees that stood sentry over the property. The sun hung high in the sky, the beams bouncing off the water and up into the canopy of branches. Considering it was late winter, she had been blessed with good weather. Spring would arrive in a couple of weeks, and she was glad it was finally warming up. Tally couldn't see any of the other cabins, but knew they were set farther back into the tree line and hidden from view. *It really is beautiful here.* She cast her gaze back over the lake. Something in the water caught her attention. At first, she couldn't make out what it was. She squinted her eyelids, peering at the object cutting through the water. *A swimmer.* Tally watched the figure draw closer, the yellow swim cap making it easy to keep track of their movement through the gentle lapping of the lake. *Looks like a woman.* Her arms were thin but lean, her shoulder muscles bunching as she pulled through each stroke. Hardly any water was thrown up from the kicking legs. *She looks like a professional.* The woman wasn't far out now. Tally could see wisps of black hair peeking out from the edge of the cap. The woman lifted her head, looking straight in front, then stopped her stroke. She turned around and began to swim back the other way. Tally watched for five more minutes, her gaze transfixed on the woman's upper back. *She's very powerful. I wonder if I'll ever be that graceful again.* One of her favourite things to do was to go for a long run. She had competed in a few marathons over the years. Now, with her pelvis and leg in ruins, her hopes of jogging once more were in tatters. *I'll be lucky if I even get back to work.* To be a police officer she needed to be physically fit. *Right now, I'm nowhere near that.*

Tally stepped away from the window and picked up the receiver sitting on the sideboard. She pressed One and waited. The call was answered on the fifth ring.

"Leighton Lake." Selma's voice came out in a rush, almost like she had raced to the phone.

"Hi, Selma. It's Tally."

"Oh, hi. Did you have a nice sleep?"

"Yes, it was very comfy, thank you. I was wondering if you could get my bags sent up. There's no hurry, but I'm up now, so whenever you can."

"Not a problem. It might be about a half hour or so. I'm knee deep in the laundry at the moment, and Fredrick and Steve are out fixing a fence."

"That's okay. I'll sit out on the deck and enjoy the afternoon sun."

Tally replaced the receiver and stepped through the door. The sun instantly warmed her face and bear arms. She leaned the crutch up against the cabin and took a few steps to the lounger that lay facing the lake. Her hip twinged, as she lowered herself to the cushion. She grabbed her trouser leg and lifted her leg onto the chair, then shifted herself up so she lay against the backrest. She let out a long breath, her body relaxing into her surroundings and she closed her eyes. *Yep, this is definitely much better than staring at the walls in my flat.* Without meaning to, she drifted off to sleep.

†

Tally stirred. A slight, cool breeze blew across her skin, raising the hairs on her arms. She opened her eyes and locked her gaze with a woman who stood at the bottom of the steps. "Hello."

"I wasn't sure how long I should wait for you to wake up. Mum said you wanted your suitcases."

Tally sat up, rubbing the sleep from her eyes. "Sorry. I must have dozed off. Have you been waiting long?"

"A few minutes."

"You must be Caitlyn."

"Yeah."

Caitlyn did not attempt to climb the steps. She kept glancing at the ground as if she were embarrassed that she caught Tally asleep. Tally grinned. Selma had a big

30

personality, but apparently, that trait hadn't been passed on to her daughter. Caitlyn's hair was damp at the ends, and Tally instinctively knew she was the woman she'd seen swimming in the lake. She refrained from looking her up and down.

"Thanks for bringing my stuff." Tally steadily got to her feet, with the help of her crutch, and took a few steps forward.

"No, you stay there. I'll bring them in for you."

"You don't have to."

"I want to."

"Okay." Tally smiled and held open the door for Caitlyn, who walked past, a case in each hand.

"Where do you want them?"

"The blue one has my clothes in it. That can go in the bedroom. The red one contains food. The kitchen is fine for that." Tally leaned against the breakfast bar that separated the kitchen from the living room, watching as Caitlyn did her bidding. Caitlyn hoisted the red case onto the kitchen counter and unzipped it. "You don't have to do that."

Caitlyn glanced at Tally and shrugged. "Mum said to make sure I do everything I can to help you."

Tally bit her lip, hating that Selma seemed to agree with Danielle. Tally didn't need to be coddled. However, the blush that tinted Caitlyn's cheeks endeared her to Tally. "Do you always do everything your mother says?"

"Not usually, but when it comes to guests, I don't have a choice." Caitlyn started to remove the items from the case, frowning as she did so. "You have a lot of noodles and soup in here." She looked up at Tally quickly. "Not much of a cook?"

"I can't stand up for long. Quick and easy is the way to go for the foreseeable future."

"Mum won't like it you're not eating properly."

"Then it'll be our little secret."

Caitlyn looked up again, her blush deepening. Her short T-shirt rose, as she reached up and opened a cabinet. Tally couldn't stop her gaze from zeroing in on Caitlyn's flat stomach. The faint outline of abs moved beneath a golden-brown tan. *I wonder if she sunbathes naked.* Tally shook her head, admonishing herself for staring. *It would do no good to be caught perving. Selma would whoop my butt.* Caitlyn was undeniably attractive, and not just in the looks department. She had this charming, goofy way about her. She piqued Tally's interest. *Maybe Mum was right; making friends would be fun.*

"We used to play together," Tally said. Caitlyn dropped the can she was holding, her cheeks now flaming. Tally hid her smirk at the double entendre. *She sure is easily embarrassed.*

"I don't remember you. But that's not surprising, what with the accident and all."

Tally raised her brows. "Accident?"

Caitlyn stopped unloading the cans and narrowed her eyes at Tally. "You don't know?"

"Know what?"

"I thought for sure your mum would have told you. Maybe my mum didn't mention it to her. But that seems strange, what with them being best friends. Perhaps she was too upset by it, but surely she would have wanted support during that time. Not that I knew what was happening back then—"

"Caitlyn."

"Maybe she was uncomfortable by it all."

"Caitlyn, you're rambling."

"What? Oh, sorry. Sometimes my thoughts get away from me." She zipped up the case and placed it on the floor. She opened another cabinet and began stacking the noodles.

"The accident?"

"It doesn't matter. Ancient history." She reached out and grabbed the door, pulling it closed. It caught the side of her head as she did so. "Shit, ow." She bent her head and rubbed the sore spot.

Tally stood and came around the bar. "Let me see."

"It's fine."

"Let me check." Tally moved Caitlyn's hand away and took another step forward, bringing her within inches of Caitlyn. Tally could smell traces of the lake on her skin. The scent mixed with Caitlyn's natural aroma made her stomach clench. Caitlyn gazed up at her, eyes wide. Tally concentrated on examining the small bump on Caitlyn's head, just behind her hairline. She threaded her fingers through Caitlyn's hair, moving it out of the way so she could see better. Her breath caught. Three inches behind where Caitlyn had hit her head lay a thick scar that ran in an arc and disappeared behind the back of her head. Tally inched back, locking gazes with Caitlyn. "What hap—"

"There we go, all done." Caitlyn nudged past Tally and rushed to the door.

"Wait."

"Enjoy your evening." Caitlyn grasped the door handle and pulled furiously, but the door wouldn't open.

"Push."

Caitlyn glanced at Tally, then lowered her head, but not before Tally caught the reddening of her cheeks. Caitlyn pushed the door open and was out of sight by the time Tally reached the threshold. She wanted to run after her, to make sure she was okay. Really, it was none of her business why Caitlyn had a giant scar. *That must have come from the accident she mentioned.* Tally went to her room and grabbed her mobile from the dresser. She pulled up her mother's contact details and dialled.

"Hey, Mum."

"Tallulah. Glad you finally decided to call."

"Sorry. Once I got here, I just wanted to rest. I've not been awake long."

Danielle sighed. "It's okay, I'm just worried about you."

"I'm fine. It's nice down here."

"Has much changed?"

Tally went to the lounge window, ignoring the pull in her pelvis, and gazed out across the lake. In the distance, she could just make out the main house. She wondered if Caitlyn was in there now, upset Tally had seen her past injury. It was clear she hadn't wanted to talk about it. She'd been quite happy to mention the accident when Tally brought up them being friends as kids and Caitlyn thought she already knew. Once it became apparent Tally had no idea what she was talking about, Caitlyn had clammed up.

"Everything is exactly how it's always been," Tally said.

"How does Selma look?"

"Still younger than you."

Danielle laughed. "She does have good genes. I've always been jealous of her looks."

"You're just as beautiful, Mum."

"Liar. Anyway, your father has finalised the plans for the cruise. We're leaving in three days. You have until then to change your mind and come home. After that, we'll be in the middle of the Caribbean. You won't be able to get hold of us unless it's an emergency."

"Go and enjoy yourselves. I'm more than happy here." For one thing, I want to find out more about Caitlyn. She looked mortified when I touched her scar. "Can I ask you something?"

"Of course."

Tally gingerly sat on the couch and laid her crutch on the floor. "I met Caitlyn today."

"Oh, good. I've not seen her in years. Is she as nice as I remember?"

"Um, yeah, but a bit skittish."

"Skittish?"

"Yeah." The whole time Caitlyn had been in the cabin, it was clear she was uncomfortable. She had a twitchy sense to her movements. Tally thought it was nerves, but now she wondered if there was something else going on. "She brought my bags in for me and unloaded the food in the cupboards."

"That was nice of her."

"Yeah. She hit her head on one of the doors. When I checked to make sure she wasn't bleeding, I noticed a rather large scar wrapping around her head." Danielle didn't comment. If not for the sound of her breathing, Tally would have thought she'd hung up. "Mum? What's going on?"

"I thought you knew."

"Knew what?"

"About the accident."

This is getting ridiculous, she's as vague as Caitlyn. "What accident?"

Danielle sighed. "When Caitlyn turned twenty, she and her brother went to visit their father for the weekend. As he was driving up the motorway, a Porsche raced past. Karl didn't like to be outdone by anyone. He put his foot down and raced after that Porsche."

"Oh, God." Tally knew where this was going. She wasn't sure she wanted to hear the rest.

"Caitlyn doesn't remember much about what happened. The police had to piece it all together from witnesses and the traffic cameras. A tyre blew out on the driver's side of Karl's car. With the speed he was going, he couldn't control the skid. The car flipped and got hit by a minibus. Karl was killed instantly."

Tally felt a tear trickle down her cheek. Her heart broke for Selma and Caitlyn. "How come you never told me? Or Selma when I saw her."

"Back then, you were partway through your military training. You were also overseas for a lot of the time, doing different courses. When you came back, four years later, I never thought to bring it up. I guess Selma doesn't like to talk about it."

"I was here twelve years ago. I asked how they all were. Selma said everyone was fine."

"Tallulah, we all deal with grief in different ways. And if I remember rightly, you went down there with a load of your friends. I doubt Selma wanted to get into that tragic part of her life with you all there."

"I suppose." Tally agreed with her mother, but still couldn't believe Selma wouldn't have said anything. *Then again, I hardly remember Karl or Caitlyn. I can't blame Selma for not mentioning it.* "So, that's where Caitlyn got her scar from?"

"Yes. She was in a coma for weeks. The doctors weren't sure she'd make it."

"That's so tragic."

"There's worse still. When Caitlyn woke up, all her memories were gone. She didn't know anything. Over time, some of them came back, but she's never been the same since."

"She seems normal enough." A little anxious, but not a freak or anything.

"She *is* normal. She's just missing parts of her life."

"I guess I should feel lucky. Things could have been a lot worse for me."

"I think you've suffered plenty."

"We all have." Tally glanced at her lap, her mind bringing up images of the X-rays that showed all the pins now holding her shattered pelvis and thigh in place. She didn't know if she would ever walk normally again. If she did have lasting effects, her job in the police force would be in jeopardy. *I refuse to be stuck behind a desk.* Tally had always been one for adventure. First the military, then pounding the streets as an officer of the law. She thrived on the danger, not knowing what might happen in any situation. Sitting behind a desk for the rest of her life would drive her crazy. "I guess that explains why Caitlyn ran out of here like her ass was on fire."

"It hasn't been an easy time for her. From what Selma told me, Caitlyn's brain works differently now. She has trouble concentrating, flits from one thing to the next. Selma said she hasn't watched a movie in years. She loses interest quickly."

That also explains her jittery behaviour. How awful for her. "I still don't understand why you never mentioned it. Even when I told you I would be staying here."

"It's been so long that it doesn't even cross my mind."

Tally didn't buy her mother's explanation but resigned herself to the knowing it was all she was going to get out of her. "Thank you for telling me now. It'll give me a heads-up when I see Caitlyn again."

"Tally, if she ran out of the cabin, she obviously doesn't want to talk about it. Leave her to tell you if she wants to. It's not your place to ask."

Tally drew in a breath, knowing Danielle was right. No one should be forced to disclose something if they weren't ready. "You're right. I won't. I'm getting hungry. I'll call you before you leave for the cruise."

"Okay. Look after yourself."

"I will. I love you."

"Love you too."

Tally disconnected and tossed the phone next to her. She leaned her head back onto the cushion and closed her eyes. Images of a battered and bruised Caitlyn came to mind. *How horrendous to wake up and not remember anything.* Tally couldn't think of anything worse. *And she lost her brother. She must have been so distraught back then.*

CHAPTER FOUR

Caitlyn rubbed her eyes, then looked back at the monitor. It was coming up to seven in the evening, and she had been staring at the screen for the better part of three hours. She knew she should take a break, but the thought of going outside turned her stomach. She didn't want to chance running into Tally. Caitlyn had been mortified when Tally's fingers brushed the hard, rigid line of her scar. The horrified look in Tally's eyes had sent Caitlyn running from the cabin. *And how embarrassing was it I couldn't open that damn door? She must think I'm a right dork.* Caitlyn had assumed Tally knew all about Karl and the accident. Their mothers had been friends for forty years. Why Danielle or Selma never told Tally was anyone's guess. Not that it mattered,

Caitlyn didn't plan on getting friendly with her anyway. *Especially after she nearly caught me drooling over her.*

When Caitlyn approached the cabin, she had seen Tally stretched out on the lounger. Not wanting to wake her, Caitlyn switched off the cart and travelled the last few metres on foot. Tally looked like a sleeping amazon. Her bare arms showed off tightly bound muscles in contrast with blonde hair gently tousled on the cushion behind her head. Caitlyn noted that strong jaw again, and legs that went on forever. She could see Tally's thigh muscles through the fabric of the trousers she wore. She was a sight to behold and had stopped Caitlyn in her tracks. She knew Tally was strong. Caitlyn still felt sore from knocking her over earlier that day. Seeing her dozing in the afternoon sun lent a quiet beauty to her strength. Caitlyn had never seen a more attractive woman.

When Tally opened her eyes, Caitlyn was transfixed. She had blushed profusely and stuttered like a crazy woman. *I'm so uncool.* In the space of fifteen minutes, Caitlyn had embarrassed herself at least three times. *And then she saw that bloody scar. She probably thinks I'm a freak.*

"Cait? You in here?" Selma asked. Caitlyn glanced over her shoulder, as the office door opened. Selma poked her head in and smiled. "There you are. I thought you'd be finished by now."

"Nearly. I just wanted to check over the next couple of months of bookings."

"Why? You did that yesterday."

Caitlyn shrugged. "It never hurts to double-check."

Selma placed a hand on Caitlyn's shoulder and peered over at the monitor. "It all looks good. Come on, dinner's ready."

"I'll be there in a minute."

"What's going on?" Selma settled a hip on the edge of the desk. "You've been holed up in here for hours."

"Nothing. Just want to make sure everything is running smoothly." Selma reached over and stilled the hand Caitlyn had on the mouse. Caitlyn sighed and straightened in the chair. "Tally saw my scar."

"Oh? How did that come about?"

"I took the cases to her as you asked. I banged my head, and she wanted to check I hadn't hurt myself." Caitlyn purposefully left out the way Tally's skin smelled like summer rain, and how those long fingers in her hair felt electric. "She lifted my hair out of the way and saw it."

"Did she upset you? What did she say?" Selma's eyes darkened as if ready for battle.

"I didn't give her the chance to say anything. I left before she could question me."

"Well, I don't know why you're hiding in here."

"She doesn't know about the accident. I was embarrassed."

"What?"

"Before I hit my head, she mentioned that we used to play together. I told her I didn't remember, but that wasn't surprising because of what happened." Caitlyn looked up at Selma. "She had no clue. I unpacked her food, hit my head, and left." Caitlyn watched her mother closely. Selma gazed off into the distance, her eyes crinkling, as she squinted and pursed her lips. "If you and Dee are such good friends, why doesn't Tally know?" Selma stood and took a few steps away. "What's going on, Mum?"

"Nothing is going on. Perhaps Dee just forgot to tell her."

Caitlyn stood forcibly, causing the desk chair to roll into the far wall. "You don't just forget that your best friend's son died and her daughter is in a coma. I deserve to know the truth."

"There is no truth. I don't know what Dee's reasons were for not telling Tally."

"You're lying."

Selma sighed and took Caitlyn's hands. "Honey, I promise you, nothing is going on. Now, forget all this. Let's go have dinner."

Caitlyn glared at Selma and snatched her hands back. There was no doubt in her mind that something more was going on. *Why would it be a secret?* "I'm not hungry. I've got a headache. I'll see you in the morning." She stormed past Selma, up the stairs to her room, and slammed the door behind her. Selma and Dee were hiding something. Caitlyn knew she wouldn't get any answers from her mother. Her next best bet would be to talk to Tally. It would mean telling her about the accident, but, at this point, she didn't care. She would find out the truth, no matter what. *Let's hope I don't make a fool out of myself again.* As she lay on her bed, her mind spun all sorts of scenarios. Whatever it was, it involved Tally in some way. *Why else would they keep it from her?*

†

Caitlyn swirled the milk with her spoon, watching the chocolate from the Weetos turn the white liquid to chocolaty brown. Head resting in her hand, her thoughts were just as jumbled as the night before. She hadn't seen Selma yet, and she wasn't looking forward to it. She still couldn't fathom why no one had told Tally of the accident. *If only I could remember what happened that day.* No matter how hard she tried, she couldn't pick up one single memory. *Perhaps I'm*

42

overthinking it all, reading too much into it. Dee could have forgotten to tell Tally. It's not like Mum and she have been overly close these last few years.

"You haven't been swimming."

Caitlyn jumped at hearing Selma's voice, and her spoon clattered to the table. She glanced up. "Wasn't feeling it today."

Selma sat at her usual spot, day planner in front of her. She quirked an eyebrow. "In all the years you've been here, I can count on one hand the times you haven't gone. What's up?"

"Nothing. Just have a bit of a headache." She picked her spoon back up and loaded it with the soggy Weetos.

"If there's something you want to talk about, I'm here."

Caitlyn shook her head. "I'm fine. What do you want me to do today?" There would be no point questioning her mother again. She would only shrug off Caitlyn's concerns. If Caitlyn wanted to find out the truth, she would have to figure it out behind Selma's back.

"Fredrick and Steve will be finishing the fence, then checking the lake for rubbish." Selma's gaze scanned the planner in front of her. "The guests in Four are checking out at ten. If you could clean the cabin and change the sheets, that would be great. Also, the hedges around Cabins Six and Three need trimming back."

"Okay. Anything else?"

"Nothing major. I'm going to be in the office most of the day, doing paperwork and updating the website. If you could be my eyes and ears out there, I'd appreciate it."

"Cool." Caitlyn stood and took her bowl to the sink. "I'll make a start on the hedges. That'll give the guests time to check out before I clean the cabin." She walked through the kitchen and out the back door without saying anything more. Selma wasn't stupid, she had noticed Caitlyn wasn't her usual chirpy self. *I need to find out the truth before she starts badgering me.*

She walked over to the tool shed. The large brick building housed all the gardening equipment, tools, and broken appliances Fredrick used for spare parts. She stepped inside, switched on the light, and headed for the hand tools. She ignored the electric trimmer and picked up the hand shears, her preferred tool. She found the manual clipping helped burn off some of her energy. She grabbed a broom, a pair of gloves, and an old wheelie bin, and loaded it all onto the golf cart. Within minutes, she was driving up the track to Cabin Six.

She parked the cart and unloaded the items. She walked around the cabin, taking a mental note of which parts of the hedges needed tidying up. As she reached the front of the cabin, her gaze scanned the lake through the trees. She thought she would have felt adrift this morning, missing the feel of the ice-cold water against her skin and the burn of her lungs as she pushed herself faster across the surface.

There was nothing.

For the first time in years, the pull of the lake was absent. Caitlyn shook her head. *I hope it doesn't stay that way.* Her mind was already flitting from one thought to the next, never settling on one thing. She knew, before long, her body would follow suit and it would be filled with a restless energy she wouldn't be able to control. *And that's when accidents happen.* She eyed the lake again. *Maybe after I finish cleaning Cabin Four I could force myself to take a swim.*

Caitlyn turned to the right, her gaze zeroing in on Cabin Seven, despite the trees that tried to obscure her view. The cabin was a few hundred yards away, but easy to spot, as it sat only a few feet from the shoreline. She took a few steps into the trees, eyes trained on the porch. Tally stood leaning against the railing, her hands cradling a mug, as she stared out over the lake. Even from this distance, Caitlyn could see the smile on her lips. Her heart rate picked up. She stepped behind a large oak, hoping to hide from Tally, and peered around the trunk. *What am I doing?* Feeling like a stalker, she stepped back, intent on getting on with her work. She glanced over her shoulder, wanting just one more look at Tally in the early morning light. Tally straightened, turned on her heal, and to Caitlyn's horror, crumpled to the decking.

Shit.

Caitlyn ran through the trees, jumped into the cart, and tore away from Cabin Six. Her pulse hammered in her chest, and the wind stung her cheeks as she sped along the track as fast as the cart would allow. "Come on," she urged. The cart wasn't built for speed, and she cursed the slowness.

The cabin came into view. Tally had one hand on the railing, the other against her hip. Her bottom lip was pulled between straight, white teeth, eyes screwed shut.

Caitlyn stopped the cart and raced up the steps. "Are you okay?" Caitlyn knelt next to Tally. She cupped her shoulder. "Tally?"

Tally lifted her head, her eyes wet with unshed tears. "I'm such an idiot."

"Of course you're not." Caitlyn's gaze roamed over Tally, at a loss at what to do. "Should I call an ambulance?"

"No! No, I'll be fine. I just need a minute."

Caitlyn moved back, sitting on her heels. From the sweat beading on Tally's forehead, it was clear she was in agony. "What if you've hurt yourself further?"

"I said I'm fine."

Caitlyn flinched. "Sorry. I'm just trying to help." She got to her knees, feeling ridiculous for rushing over. "I'm sorry." She attempted to stand, but Tally gripped her hand.

"No, I'm sorry." She looked away. "I sometimes forget that I'm not as strong as I once was. I would be very grateful if you could help me up."

"Okay." Caitlyn looked around. "Where are your crutches?"

"Inside."

Caitlyn stood and found them slung in the fireplace. She frowned and shook her head. She had only met Tally a couple of times, but it was obvious Tally didn't like feeling weak. She didn't know anything about her, but even she could tell Tally was used to being in control. *I wonder what happened to her.* She retrieved the sticks and went back outside. Tally was now leaning against the spindles, her chest rising and falling rapidly, as she breathed deeply. Caitlyn raised the crutches, her brows lifting in unison.

Tally's cheeks tinted pink. "I got frustrated last night. I didn't want to deal with them."

"So you thought you'd burn them?"

Tally shrugged. "Couldn't find a damn match."

Caitlyn chuckled and sat opposite Tally. "Do you suppose you should maybe keep them around for a bit longer?"

Tally sighed, glancing at the crutches that lay in between them. She looked back at Caitlyn. "I'm not used to depending on anyone or anything. It's been months now, and I still can't walk properly." Tally looked skyward. "Some days, I don't think I'll ever be normal again."

Caitlyn understood that emotion all too well. It was hard losing her memories from before the accident, but at least she had nothing to compare herself with. Tally didn't have that luxury. She knew exactly who she was then. *Seeing yourself as a weaker version must be horrendous.* "What is normal? Perhaps, instead of thinking of yourself as abnormal, you should just think of yourself as a different version. Not better, not worse. Just different."

"Does that work for you?"

Caitlyn locked gazes with Tally, the intensity of her stare made her heart catch. "You know, don't you?"

Tally nodded. "After you ran out yesterday, I called my mum."

"What did she tell you?" Caitlyn had wanted to speak to Tally about this, but she didn't know that conversation would be happening so soon.

"You and your brother were in a car accident. He died and you were in a coma. You lost your memory."

"Yep. That pretty much sums it up."

"I'm sorry. That must have been a very emotional time."

Caitlyn gazed over at the lake, the ripples twinkling in the sunshine. "It was horrible. My brother had died, and I couldn't even remember him. I still don't, not really." She looked back at Tally. "Can I ask you something?"

"Sure."

"How come you never knew? Our mothers are best friends. Why wouldn't Dee tell you what happened?"

"I had the same thought yesterday. I even came to stay here twelve years ago. That would have been a couple of years after it happened. No one said anything."

"Why do you think that is?"

47

Tally glanced at the decking boards beneath her, her shoulders dropping as she sighed. "I don't know, but I think they're hiding something."

"That's what I thought, too. I have no idea what, though. I can't remember anything about the accident, only what Mum told me."

"What about the police? Surely they would have questioned you."

"Yes, once I woke up, but I had nothing to say. I didn't know anything. Not even my name. Everything I know came from Mum."

"What do you want to do about it?"

"How do you mean?"

"I don't know if you know, but I'm a police officer. I can probably find out about the accident."

Caitlyn shook her head. "I already know what happened there. Karl chased a car and our tyre blew out."

"That's what you were told. What if it's something different?"

Caitlyn hadn't thought of that. She had only been thinking that Tally had been involved somehow. Selma lying about the events of that day never entered her mind.

Caitlyn's body trembled.

"What is it?" Tally placed her hand on Caitlyn's knee.

"I just assumed the facts of the accident were true and that you were the mystery. You were the only one who didn't know about the accident. But what if they lied to hide the true nature of the accident, and no one told you because they didn't want me finding out the truth?"

"That's possible. It would make sense. They must have known I would see you at some point, so keeping it from me would guarantee you wouldn't find out."

Caitlyn stood and rubbed her forehead. Her pulse pounded behind her eyes. "What could they be hiding?"

"Caitlyn?"

"Yeah?"

"Can we talk about this inside? My hip is screaming at me."

"Oh, shit. Sorry." Caitlyn passed the crutches to Tally, then gripped under Tally's armpits and lifted with all her strength. It was a struggle to get Tally off the ground. *She is so buff.* Caitlyn shook the thought away. Together, they got her to her feet. Caitlyn lightly touched Tally's back, as she guided her through the door and onto the sofa. "Can I get you anything? Tablets or something."

"No thanks. They make me sleepy. The pain will subside in a minute. Sit."

Caitlyn sat on the edge of the sofa next to Tally's outstretched legs, her gaze fixed on the floorboards. *Mum lied to me. All these years.* She swallowed hard, fearing she'd throw up. *But why?*

"You're upset," Tally said.

"Yes. I don't understand what's going on."

"Do you want me to look into the accident?"

"Why would you do that? You don't even know me."

"I did, once. The police side of me wants to know what's going on, because finding the truth is what I do. But I also want to help you. It's clear how much this is hurting you. Tell me what you need me to do."

Caitlyn gazed up into Tally's eyes, finding nothing but strength and compassion. The intensity of her gaze made her want to cry. "There's no point in asking Mum. She won't tell me the truth. If you could find out what happened that day, I would truly appreciate it."

One side of Tally's mouth pulled up in a half smile. "I'll see what I can do."

"Thank you."

"I can't promise anything, but I'll try my best."

"Are you sure you should be doing this? You're supposed to be resting and getting better."

"It's just a few phone calls. It won't interrupt my recovery."

Caitlyn glanced down at Tally's hip and pelvis. The urge to ask what had happened pulled strong at her inquisitive mind. She bit her lip and looked away.

"That's a story for another day."

Caitlyn whipped her head around. "I wasn't going to ask."

"I know, but I know you're curious."

"You don't have to tell me."

"It's not a secret, but it is hard to talk about."

Caitlyn waved her hand. "It's fine. I don't need to know, and I would never expect you to tell me anything you didn't want to."

"As I said, a story for another time."

"Okay. I should get back to work. Mum will go mad if she finds me skiving." She stood and straightened her shorts. Looking back up, she caught Tally staring at her thighs, tongue peeking out between moist lips. *She's checking me out.* Caitlyn refrained from smiling, although it was good to know she had some effect on Tally. *Lord knows she gets me going.* "Thank you for helping me."

Tally's head shot up, a blush working its way up her neck. "What? Oh, no problem. I'll let you know when I find something. And thank you for helping me up. I'm embarrassed to have you see me like that, but I'm glad you were there to help."

"I would say anytime, but I'd prefer it if you used the crutches from now on."

"Yes, ma'am." Tally grinned.

"Good. I'll leave you to it. Have a nice day."

"You, too. Oh, Caitlyn?"

Caitlyn stopped at the threshold, hand on the doorknob. "Yeah?"

"I have a physiotherapist coming tomorrow about ten thirty. Will there be someone at the desk to show her the way?"

"I'll make sure of it."

"Thank you."

Caitlyn climbed into the cart and set off back to Cabin Six at a leisurely pace. She hadn't meant to get into the accident but was pleased it had come up. Her only concern had been to reach Tally in case she had hurt herself. As it turned out, she now had an ally. She wasn't sure how she would be able to act normally around Selma. The thought that she may have lied to her all this time turned Caitlyn's stomach. She was terrified of what Tally might find out. Not knowing was worse. Just because she couldn't remember a good chunk of her life, didn't mean she didn't deserve to know the truth.

CHAPTER FIVE

Tally looked out over the lake and toward the sun just beginning its ascent in the sky beyond the trees. The chilly morning breeze raised the hair on her arms, but she wasn't cold. She took a deep breath. Filling her lungs with the crisp, clean air felt wonderful. This was her second morning on the lake, and she already felt more relaxed than she ever had living in the city. The only sounds were of the branches swaying and the birds tweeting. The occasional moo could be heard off into the distance. It had been hard to get to sleep the first night. Lying in complete silence with no traffic noise to lull her to slumber had felt weird. Last night, she had drifted off without trouble. And her pelvis and hip didn't seem to bother her as much this morning.

She scanned the surrounding trees, looking for signs of life. There was no movement anywhere on the shoreline. In the very far distance, she could just see the faint glow of a light on in the main house. Tally wondered if Caitlyn was awake. *Caitlyn.* Tally smiled, picturing her in her mind. Tally had been mortified when she fell to the ground and Caitlyn had appeared from nowhere. She had been so busy trying not to cry, she hadn't noticed Caitlyn's arrival. A gentle touch on her shoulder made Tally realise she wasn't alone. *I wonder where she was when I fell. She must have been watching me.* The thought should have unnerved her, but she found it oddly comforting. Caitlyn was a very attractive woman. It was no surprise Tally was drawn to her. *She seems so sweet, so innocent. The look on her face when she realised she had been lied to by Selma was heartbreaking.* Tally had wondered all day what could have happened for there to be this big secret. She was determined to do whatever she could to help Caitlyn. After her physio, she would ring her partner back at the force and see if he could find out what happened. She hoped with all her heart it was nothing and they were both just overthinking it all. *Mum really could have just forgotten to mention it.* Tally didn't believe that for a second, but she would wait before passing judgment on them.

Tally's gaze scanned the water again. In the distance, a familiar figure came into view. The sunbeams bounced off the yellow swim cap, creating a halo effect around Caitlyn's head. Powerful arms propelled her through the ripples. Tally gripped the railing tight in her hands, mesmerised by the strength Caitlyn possessed in the water. *She looks like she belongs in the sea, like a graceful mermaid.* On land, Caitlyn had a nervous energy about her, but in the lake, all traces of her jumpiness were absent.

Tally kept a watchful eye, as Caitlyn swam the perimeter of the lake. Before long, she was only a few yards away. Her head came out of the water, her gaze finding Tally. Tally waved. Caitlyn changed direction and headed for the shore. She stood in the shallows and walked up the gravel embankment. Tally couldn't stop her gaze from drifting down Caitlyn's body. She wore a red Speedo swimsuit, the cut of the fabric rising high over her hips. Water droplets ran in rivulets down her skin and merged with the earth. Tally swallowed hard, her pulse hammering in her chest. *Dear Lord, she's gorgeous.*

Caitlyn stopped at the base of the steps, gazing up at Tally, who still clung to the railing. "Good morning."

"Aren't you cold out in the lake?" Tally wet her lips, as she glimpsed the outline of Caitlyn's nipples poking through the swimsuit.

"Initially, yes, but once I get going, I don't notice it. You should try it sometime."

Tally shook her head. "No way. I like to be adventurous, but I don't fancy freezing my butt off."

"By the time you leave here, I'll have you swimming with me every morning."

"We'll see." Tally's laugh came out as a snort. Seeing Caitlyn in next to nothing was turning her on, a long-forgotten sensation. She wasn't sure if Annabelle had ever made her feel so inept. Tally was usually the confident one, but staring at Caitlyn had her all mixed up and confused. "How are you feeling after yesterday?"

Caitlyn shrugged. "I'm okay. I'm trying to avoid my mother as much as possible. I'm glad I talked to you about it. It's nice to not feel so alone with it all."

"Anytime. I'm going to call my buddy later today and see if he can find out what happened. It might take him a while, though."

"That's okay. It's been fourteen years. A bit longer won't hurt." Caitlyn's body shivered, so she wrapped her arms around her waist. "I need to get back in there." She motioned to the water with a tilt of her head.

"Okay. See you around."

"By the way, we made a deal."

Tally raised her eyebrows. "Did we?"

"Yes. Where are your crutches?"

Tally felt heat rise to her cheeks. She glanced away. "They're in the bedroom. But I'm feeling okay today."

Caitlyn pursed her lips. "Do me a favour. I know you might feel you don't need them, but could you at least carry one with you? I don't want you hurting yourself."

Tally wanted to huff in protest. She hated that people thought they knew what was best for her, but the concern in Caitlyn's eyes made her relent. "Okay. But only because you asked so nicely."

Caitlyn smirked, then turned away. As she strode back into the water, Tally couldn't help but watch every twitch of her ass cheeks. Tally was in danger of falling for Caitlyn, and that was something she wasn't prepared for. She had come to the lake to focus on her recovery. Still, she found herself more and more intrigued after each meeting with Caitlyn.

Tally watched her swim away until she was a mere speck in the distance. *What am I doing? I hardly know her, but there is something about her that's keeping me interested.* She turned away from the lake and limped back inside. She headed into the bedroom, spying the crutches leaning up against the dresser. She narrowed her eyes at them. She hated being dependant on them. She sighed and picked one up, threading her arm through the loop and grasping the handle. *I did promise her. Hopefully, the physiotherapist will work her magic and I can soon be rid of them.*

She went to the kitchen and made herself another coffee, glancing at the old grandfather clock standing sentry by the lounge window. The physiotherapist would arrive in just over two hours. Coffee cup in one hand and crutch in the other, Tally made her way out onto the deck to continue watching the birth of the day.

†

Tally opened her eyes at the sound of gravel crunching under tyres near the deck. She turned her head, as a dark-blue Jeep rolled to a stop. She recognised Selma sitting in the passenger seat, one hand gripping the door frame. Tally got to her feet and waved. She hadn't seen Selma since being deposited at the cabin upon arrival. As far as she knew, Caitlyn hadn't mentioned to Selma her concerns over her accident, so Tally was unsure how to act around her. *Block it out of your mind. You don't want Selma finding out you're looking into her past.* She turned her gaze to the other woman in the driver's seat. Her hair was braided into a French plait, her skin tanned a deep golden brown. As she stepped from the car, Tally caught sight of firm calves and muscled thighs peeking out from under the cargo shorts.

"Good morning, Tally," Selma said.

Tally looked back to Selma. "Good morning. Lovely day, isn't it?"

Selma smiled, tilting her head back to look up at the clear blue sky. "It always is around here."

Tally agreed with that statement. She had no doubt that even in bad weather, the lake and surrounding trees were just as beautiful.

"This is Emma. Caitlyn said you were expecting a visitor."

Tally nodded and glanced back to the newcomer, who was lifting a fold-out table from the back of the Jeep. "Yes, thank you for showing her the way."

"No problem." Selma took a step away, but then looked back. "Caitlyn told me you don't have much here in the way of proper food. Come to the main house tonight for dinner. Around seven."

Tally didn't get a chance to argue, as Selma strode away. She frowned. The last thing she wanted to do was sit around a table with Selma, knowing Selma and Danielle had lied to Caitlyn. *Then again, Caitlyn will probably be there.* She smiled, thinking how nice it would be to get to know her better.

She turned her attention back to Emma, who was lugging the table and a duffle bag up the decking steps. "Can I help with anything?"

"Thanks, but I'm okay." Emma made it up onto the porch, dropped her bag, and held out her hand. "I'm Emma Grant."

"Tally. Nice to meet you." They shook hands, Emma's grip firm in her own. *My gaydar is pinging.* "Thank you for agreeing to come out to see me. I hope it's not too much trouble."

"None at all. I quite often do home visits. Shall we?" Emma nodded to the door.

Tally opened the door and followed Emma in. Emma glanced around quickly, then set the table up in the centre of the lounge. She reached into her duffle, pulled out a sheet, and laid it over the table.

"I've got notes here from the hospital and your GP. If you go change into a dressing gown or something, I'll just refresh my memory." She pulled a folder from her bag and opened it.

Tally glanced down at her jogging bottoms, frowning. She didn't own a dressing gown. "Would a towel be okay?"

Emma looked up from the file she was leafing through. "Whatever you're comfortable in. I need to check the incision sites, and be able to manipulate your leg and hip. Anything that's not restrictive is fine."

Tally nodded and limped into the bedroom, leaving her crutch in the living room. She stripped off her joggers, leaving her underwear on, and wrapped a large towel around her lower half. Her skin heated at the thought of this stranger seeing her half naked. Tally wasn't shy, not by any means. Plenty of doctors and nurses had seen her undressed in the last few months, but this was someone new. She shook the embarrassment away, knowing that Emma wouldn't be viewing her body in a personal way. To Emma, Tally was just a bunch of muscles, tendons, and skin that needed fixing. Holding the towel tightly around her waist, she went back to the lounge.

Emma looked up as Tally entered. "If you hop up onto the table, I'll go through what I have planned, then I'll check the wounds and your mobility. We won't be doing much this session."

"Okay." Tally made her way to the table. She braced her hands on the edge of the padding and shifted herself up and back, grimacing as her hip pulled against her pelvis."

Emma narrowed her eyes. "That hurt, I assume?"

Tally nodded. "Yes. Around my hip joint."

Emma looked at the notes. "It says here your pelvis was fractured around the pubis and the ilium, and you tore the sacrospinous ligament."

"That's correct. The pubis was a clean break and the ilium broke in four places, I think, so had to be pinned together."

"But the hip socket was undamaged?"

"Yes."

"Hmm." Emma flipped over another page. "It says here you ripped the muscles around the hip joint, that might be what's causing you discomfort when you flex your leg. It's been nearly four months now hasn't it?" Tally nodded. "Your pain should be at a much lower level by now. Have you been doing the exercises the hospital suggested?"

Tally looked down at her knees. She had been lax in doing them. She had been too upset over Annabelle leaving, and had sunk into self-pity. She had hardly moved at all. She shook her head.

Emma tossed the file down onto the couch cushions, sighing as she did so. "I don't want to preach to you, but if you want to get better, you need to do what is prescribed. I imagine the muscles have begun to waste away. We need to build those back up again at the same time as getting your flexibility back and doing more weight-bearing exercises."

"I can walk a few steps, but it hurts. My leg keeps giving way."

"Describe how it happens."

"I'm usually fine going in a straight line. When I turn, it feels like my hip is popping out of the socket and I go down."

"Okay. I'll show you some exercises you can do to strengthen the muscles around your hip joint. Can you swim?"

Tally's mind flashed to Caitlyn swimming in the lake. "Yes."

"If you can get to the pool, I'd recommend doing hydrotherapy. You can strengthen your lower half without putting pressure on your joints or pelvis. Once you get stronger, you'll be able to put more weight on your leg. I also would like you to do the stretches I'm going to show you, twice a day."

"Okay."

"Right, lie back on the table, and I'll take a look."

Tally did as asked, closing her eyes as Emma moved the towel away. Emma ran cold hands over Tally's hip, waist, and thigh. Tally grimaced as her leg was lifted and moved around. The pain intensified when Emma pulled her leg to the side. A tear slipped from her eye. Emma placed her leg back down and covered her back up with the towel.

"Sorry about that."

Tally opened her eyes and attempted to smile.

"I'm a little concerned about how much pain you're still in. I'm going to request an X-ray at the hospital to check everything is where it should be. I'm hoping it's just lack of movement that's causing it, but I want to make sure. In the meantime, carry on with light stretches, but don't overdo it. I'll get you on the list and get you seen as soon as possible."

Tally swung her legs off the table and sat up, her mind whirling. No way she could ask her brother to come back out to take her to the hospital. *I'll have to get a taxi.* "Okay."

"You've done really well. Go get changed, and I'll write out what exercises I want you to do."

Tally emerged from the bedroom once again. Emma was all packed up, her stuff by the door. Over the next few minutes, Emma demonstrated the stretches to Tally, then helped her through the routine. Tally hated every minute of it and couldn't wait for Emma to leave so she could take a pain pill, lie down, and sleep. She saw Emma out onto the porch. "Thanks again for coming."

"I'll see you in five days. Make sure you do the stretches."

"I will."

Emma loaded up the car, just as Caitlyn appeared through the trees, riding the golf cart. She rolled to a stop next to the Jeep. Tally didn't miss the look of interest in Emma's eyes as she looked Caitlyn up and down. Tally drew her brows tighter and pursed her lips. It would seem she wasn't the only one who had a good gaydar. Caitlyn nodded a hello toward Emma and walked past her toward the cabin.

"I'll let you know when I get the X-ray booked," Emma called over. She glanced at Caitlyn and smirked, winking as she did so. She climbed into the car and rolled away.

Caitlyn mounted the stairs, a frown marring her usually carefree features. "I didn't know Emma was your therapist."

Tally glanced at the car as it disappeared up the track. "You know her?" The ache in her pelvis and hip forced her to go inside and search out her pain medication. Caitlyn followed. Tally opened the bottle and swallowed two pills, then limped over to the sofa. She laid her crutch on the floor beside her. Caitlyn stood just inside the doorway, chewing her lip and worrying her thumbs with her forefingers. "Caitlyn? What is it?"

Caitlyn reached into her pocket and pulled out a piece of paper and handed it over to Tally. "I realised earlier, I didn't give you the date of the accident or where it happened. This is everything I can remember. I thought you'd need it for when you ring your friend."

"Thanks." Tally took the slip of paper and put it into her pocket, unopened. She didn't want to talk about that. She wanted to know what was going on with Emma. It was clear Caitlyn wasn't too happy with her presence. If Tally were to have Emma working with her, she needed to know if there were going to be any problems. Especially if they upset Caitlyn. "How do you know Emma?" Caitlyn flinched at hearing her name but didn't answer. "Please, sit down. Talk to me."

Caitlyn glanced at Tally, then sighed. She chose to sit on the floor instead of the cushion next to Tally. "We used to date."

Tally's stomach involuntarily clenched. Images of Emma and Caitlyn together flashed through her mind. "Oh?"

"Yeah. It was a while ago."

"What happened? If you don't mind me asking." Tally wasn't sure she wanted to know. Judging by Caitlyn's stiff posture on the floor, arms wrapped tightly around her knees, the break-up wasn't pleasant.

Caitlyn shrugged, her gaze glued to Tally's knees that were inches from her own. "We dated for a few months, but I never felt settled with her." Caitlyn looked up under lowered lashes, her forehead creasing. "Since the accident, I have this restless energy. I can't keep still. My thoughts jump from one thing to the next, never staying long on one thought. My body is the same. I can be doing one thing and get distracted doing something else. The only time I don't feel like that is when I'm in the water."

"That must be difficult."

She shrugged again. "I'm used to it. It pisses Mum off sometimes when she's trying to talk to me and my mind wanders. Anyway, Emma always complained that I never could relax with her. We'd have dinner at her place and cuddle on the sofa, but I was always fidgeting. I tried to explain why I'm like that, but she wouldn't listen. I told her it would be best if we didn't see each other anymore. She said that was fine, but as you probably noticed, she still keeps flirting with me."

Tally's eyes drifted shut for a moment, the pain meds making her tired. She didn't want Caitlyn to think she didn't care, but she was finding it hard to stay awake. "I can find someone else to work with if her being here will upset you."

"You're slurring."

Tally's head fell back. She jerked upright, eyes popping open. "Meds." She felt hands cup her calves and lift her legs onto the sofa. She lay back. Caitlyn's fingers brushed hair back from her forehead, then rested on her shoulder.

"I'm okay with her being here. She's good at her job. It just took me by surprise."

"K. Long as y'sure."

"Positive. Sleep now. I'll come back in a bit and check on you."

"Don't need to."

"I want to."

Caitlyn's voice had dropped to a whisper, the tone soothing Tally deeper into sleep. She wasn't sure, but she thought she felt cool lips on her forehead.

CHAPTER SIX

Caitlyn clutched the stack of towels to her chest as she stared up at Tally's cabin door, a tremor running through her body. *I can't believe I kissed her head. What was I thinking?* When Tally drifted off, it seemed only natural for Caitlyn to lift her legs and smooth her hair. Tally was being so nice to her, listening to her ramble on about the accident and Emma. It felt like Tally genuinely cared about her. Which was strange, as they only met two days ago. Nonetheless, it was a nice feeling. Bending down to kiss her forehead didn't require thought; she just did it. *And now here I stand, terrified to go in. She must think I'm an idiot.* Caitlyn had promised to check on her, so she shook her head, took a breath, and marched up the steps. She was about to knock, when she caught sight of Tally through the glass door, thrashing around on the sofa. Caitlyn grabbed the handle and pulled the door wide. She rushed through and dropped the towels on the floor and sunk to her knees at the edge of the couch. Tally's face and neck were covered in sweat, her T-shirt askew. She groaned through tight lips, her fists clenched in the air. Caitlyn reached out and grasped her shoulder.

"Tally, wake up." Caitlyn squeezed a little tighter. She ducked, as one of Tally's fists punched out toward her. "Tally!"

Tally's eyes popped open, her gaze frantically searching the room, before settling on Caitlyn. "Help me."

The words were whispered, but Caitlyn could hear the fear in them. She didn't think. She climbed onto the sofa and wrapped one arm around Tally's shoulder, using her other hand to cradle Tally's face. It was a tight fit, but she didn't worry about falling off. Tally's grip on her was painful, but she didn't care. Whatever nightmare Tally had gone through was horrendous. There was no way Caitlyn was going anywhere.

"You're okay. You're safe. Just relax." After a few moments, Tally's ragged breathing began to settle down and her grip loosened. "That's it, just relax. I'm here." The pounding of Tally's heart against Caitlyn's side subsided so much so she could feel only breath warm against her chest. It wasn't long before Tally drifted off to sleep again. Caitlyn knew she should move but was loathe to disturb Tally. Besides, she wanted to stay there with her to make sure she wouldn't have another nightmare. As she lay still, listening to the sounds of Tally's shallow breathing, Caitlyn soon joined her in slumber.

†

Through the heavy haze of sleep, Caitlyn heard movement in the distance. The sound of a spoon moving round in a cup stirred her consciousness. She opened her eyes. Tally sat on a bar stool with said spoon in hand, still stirring whatever was in the white mug. As if sensing Caitlyn was awake, Tally glanced at her, her face instantly flushing. Caitlyn hadn't meant to fall asleep. It was strange to realise she had done that so easily. Not once had she ever been able to lie still with someone next to her. She thought of her disastrous sleepovers with Emma. Caitlyn had thought they were well suited. Emma had been the first woman in a long time to capture her interest, but Caitlyn never felt settled enough to relax in her presence. *Yet with Tally, it was effortless. What does that mean?* Caitlyn cleared her throat and sat up, running her hand through her hair as she did so. "Are you okay?" Caitlyn asked.

Tally went back to stirring her drink, her gaze troubled. "Yes. I, um, am having a little trouble figuring out why I woke up practically lying on top of you." Her blush deepened.

"You don't remember?"

Tally shook her head.

"I came to check on you as I promised. You were having a nightmare." Tally's forehead creased, still gazing at her cup. Caitlyn stood and walked toward her, the usual urge to flee absent. She sat on the stool next to Tally. "You were thrashing about, covered in sweat. I tried to wake you. I didn't know what else to do." She cleared her throat again. "I got on the sofa with you and held you. You settled down almost immediately."

Tally was quiet for a long moment, eyes narrowed, seemingly lost in thought. "I think I was dreaming about the day I was injured."

"Does that happen a lot?"

"In the beginning, it happened all the time. I haven't had one for weeks now. I guess talking about the injuries with Emma brought it all up again in my mind." Tally sighed and put the spoon down. She looked at Caitlyn. "Thank you for helping me. I'm sorry you had to do that."

Caitlyn slid her hand across the bar top and rested a light touch on Tally's wrist. "I'm not. I'm here any time you want to talk. I'm not great with advice, but I'm a good listener." *If I can sit still long enough. Though, with Tally, it seems easy. Like now, I'm not thinking of anything but her. How strange.*

"Thanks." Tally squeezed Caitlyn's hand before withdrawing her own and grasping the mug. "I'm not sure I'm up for going over what happened right now."

"You don't have to, but at any time you feel you want to talk about it, I'm here." Tally smiled, her eyes crinkling in the corners. Caitlyn took a breath and changed the subject, sensing Tally's walls going up. "How did your session go?"

"It was good. Emma showed me exercises I need to do every day. She's a little concerned that my hip is in a lot of pain. She wants me to get an X-ray to check everything is okay."

"I can take you when you need to go, if you want."

"You don't need to do that. I can get a taxi."

"The nearest hospital is fifteen miles away. That'll cost you a fortune. Besides, Mum did say I have to provide everything the guests need to make their stay as comfortable as possible."

"And here I thought it was because you cared."

Caitlyn rolled her eyes at the jibe and smiled. "If you haven't figured out yet that I care about you, then I'm doing something wrong." Caitlyn hadn't meant to be so open with her words, but Tally's shy smile and seeing her cheeks tint pink made the admission worth it.

"I care about you too."

"Is it strange we feel that way after only a couple of days?"

"Probably. Then again, the times we've talked have been pretty intense, intimate almost. I don't think there's anything wrong with that."

"I guess not. What else did Emma say?"

"She wants me to go swimming." Tally shook her head when Caitlyn smiled wide and must have read her mind. "Not on your life."

"Come on. It'll be great."

Tally shook her head vigorously. "I have no desire to dunk my head in the freezing cold water."

"You don't need to worry. We'll soon get you warmed up." Caitlyn didn't miss the widening of Tally's eyes. She realised how flirty that sounded. Thankfully, Tally didn't comment.

"No thanks. I'll take my chances in a real pool, preferably already heated."

Damn, there goes my chances of seeing her in a swimsuit. But then again... "I'm still a member of the local gym. I can take you out there as a guest. You won't have to pay to get in."

"Is this all part of the Leighton Lake guest experience?"

"Absolutely. We're very proud of our five-star rating. I'd like to keep it that way."

Tally looked away for a moment, rubbing her chin. She looked back at Caitlyn. "Are you sure you wouldn't mind? I don't want to take you away from your responsibilities here."

Caitlyn waved her off. "I don't work twenty-four hours. I've got plenty of time to go swimming with you."

Tally narrowed her eyes again. "Are you sure this isn't just a way for you to spend more time in the water?"

"Damn, you figured it out."

Tally's laugh instantly embedded itself into Caitlyn's memory bank, melodious and throaty all at the same time. It was, quite frankly, the sexiest laugh Caitlyn had ever heard.

"I swear you're part fish."

Caitlyn grinned. She was about to retort when her phone vibrated in her pocket. She pulled it free, seeing *Mum* flash on the screen. "That's Mum. I have to get back to work."

"Okay."

Caitlyn declined the call and put the phone away. She needed time to figure out what she would tell Selma as to why she had been gone so long just to replenish towels. She stood from the stool and made her way to the door. She bent and scooped up the towels and turned back to Tally. "Where do you want these?"

"Just leave them on the sofa. I'll put them away."

Caitlyn did so, then gazed back at Tally. "Did Mum invite you for dinner tonight?"

"Yeah, she did."

"Great. I'll see you later."

"See you later."

Caitlyn opened the door, the sunshine momentarily blinding her. For some reason, it felt later than it was.

"Cait?"

Caitlyn glanced over her shoulder. "Yeah?"

"Thank you, for…you know." Tally gestured to the sofa, alluding to her nightmare.

"You're welcome." She smiled and left, closing the door quietly behind her. As she drove off in the golf cart, she realised she was sporting a huge grin. Sometimes, she was clueless about women. With Tally, it was clear they held a mutual attraction for one another. If that would lead to anything, she didn't know. One thing she did know for sure, she couldn't wait to get Tally to the swimming pool. The prospect of having dinner with her that night kept her smiling for the rest of the afternoon.

CHAPTER SEVEN

Tally resisted the urge to follow Caitlyn out the door and watch her drive away. Instead, she limped back over to her vacated barstool and sat down with a sigh. She couldn't believe she had woken up on the sofa cradled in Caitlyn's arms. She'd lain there, absorbing the feeling of contentment. Caitlyn smelled like fresh air and lake water, her body warm and soft beneath her. It wasn't often that Tally felt the need to be comforted. Being that close to Caitlyn had been a welcome surprise. She hardly remembered the nightmare, not until Caitlyn had explained what happened. The last thing she remembered was drifting off while Caitlyn talked about Emma. It was good to know Caitlyn was a lesbian; at least Tally wouldn't have a crush on a straight woman.

It was still dangerous.

Knowing there might be a chance Caitlyn liked her sent a chill through Tally's body. She had come to Leighton Lake to recuperate, and now she was thinking of nothing but Caitlyn. There was a spark between them. She knew it. Such openness was rare between two people who had just met, but their connection was effortless. Her skin heated, as she remembered Caitlyn's offer to take her swimming. Tally just hoped she wouldn't drown in an attempt to swim with her bum leg. *How mortifying would it be if Caitlyn had to save me? Then again, it'll be worth it to see her in her swimsuit.*

Tally shook the thoughts from her mind and finished off her cold tea. She reached across the countertop and grabbed her mobile, while pulling the piece of paper from her pocket with her other hand. She scrolled through her contacts and selected Ryan's name. Ryan Porter had been her colleague and friend for six years. She was as close to him as she was her brother. Ryan was there the day she was injured. Lying on the cold, wet concrete, Tally had thought her life was over. She was in so much pain, she couldn't focus on anything except trying to breathe. Ryan's face came into view. His normally tan skin was pale, and his eyes were wide with fright. He made all the right calls to the emergency services, kept her calm, and reassured her everything would be fine, but Tally could see the fear in his gaze. That incident had bonded them even closer. Ryan even stayed with her and Annabelle in the first two weeks Tally came out of the hospital. That was until Annabelle asked him to go. She told Ryan she would be the only one to look after Tally. Ryan revealed the truth only after Annabelle left. If Tally had known that at the time, she would have asked Annabelle to go instead of Ryan. Not that it mattered anyway, Annabelle left only a few weeks later.

"Hey, T. Long time no hear," Ryan said, breaking Tally's morose trip down memory lane.

"I called you three days ago. Not exactly a lifetime ago."

"Yeah, well, I miss picking on you. How's the trip going?"

Caitlyn's face drew into focus, and Tally smiled. "It's good, really peaceful down here. You'd love the lake. It's huge. You should try to come down before I leave. It's amazing."

"I'd love that, but I'm not sure if I can get the time off. I've only got a couple of week's holiday left and that's booked for Christmas. If I can change some shifts around, I might be able to swing a couple of days."

"It'll be great to see you."

"I saw you six days ago, hardly a lifetime ago."

Tally laughed at his use of her own words. "Well, it's too long. I miss you."

"Yeah, yeah, yeah. What meds have they got you on now? You've gone all emotional."

Tally missed his banter. She truly believed they would be best friends forever. "Just admit you miss me too."

Ryan grunted. "I suppose. Just a little."

"Such a sweetheart. Listen, there's a reason I called you, and not just to provide a target for your sarcasm."

"What's up?" Ryan's previously playful tone changed immediately to the voice he used on the beat.

"I've met a woman down here. She's the daughter of the owner."

"The owner is your mum's friend, isn't she?"

"Yes. Caitlyn—that's the daughter's name—was involved in a serious car accident fourteen years ago. Her brother was killed, and she suffered a brain injury."

"Sounds horrible."

"Yeah, it was. Anyway, Mum and Selma—that's my Mum's friend—never told me about it. Caitlyn thinks Selma is hiding something. She can't remember any of the details about the crash, and I was hoping you could do a search through the archives to find the incident report; police statements and witnesses, etcetera."

"Sure, that's fine. It might take me a few days, though."

"As soon as you can is fine. I don't know if there will be anything useful in the report anyway, but it might put Caitlyn's mind at ease." Tally hoped so anyway. She wasn't sure Caitlyn would be able to deal with any difference between the report and Selma's version of the events. With her memory stolen from her, Caitlyn had placed all her trust in her mother, as anyone would. To find out she'd been lied to would be devastating.

"I'll email it to you the first chance I get. Text me the details, and I'll see what I can find."

"Thank Ry, you're the best."

"I know."

Tally could hear the smirk in his voice.

"T, I gotta run. Got an incident to attend to."

Tally heard the siren being switched on. Adrenalin shot through her body, an instinctive reaction to a call-out. There was nothing quite like the feeling of jumping into the unknown. Tally thrived on that feeling and wondered if she'd ever feel it again. She didn't have time to say goodbye to Ryan; the line went dead. She locked her phone and placed it back on the countertop, setting a reminder in her head to text Ryan the details he needed. With that sorted, she stood and headed for the bathroom. She had a dinner to prepare for. No way she would turn up at the main house without a shower.

She hadn't had one since arriving. She didn't even try to pretend her motivation was social politeness. She wanted to smell nice for Caitlyn. Caitlyn hadn't said anything earlier, but Tally had no doubt she'd gotten a whiff of a few days' worth of sweat. She didn't want Caitlyn thinking she smelled like that all the time. Despite having doubts she would be able to stand in the shower for a proper clean, she was determined to do her best.

†

Tally turned off the golf cart and stared up at the back of the main house. The sun hung low in the sky, casting a homely orange glow around the trees and lake. The turning of the season was right around the corner, and Tally couldn't wait for the warmer months.

Her heart pounded in her chest. She was nervous. *It's not like this is a date. Stop being stupid.* She couldn't help it. Although it had only been a few hours, her excitement at seeing Caitlyn again brought her out in a cold sweat. She rubbed her hands on her jeans, trying to dry off her clammy hands. It wasn't just seeing Caitlyn that had her anxious. This would be the first time she would be spending any proper time with Selma since her arrival. Caitlyn had said she wouldn't bring up the accident with her mother again until Tally found out the truth of what happened. That didn't stop Tally from worrying about how she would come across. She didn't want Selma to know what Caitlyn had asked of her.

She climbed from the cart and pulled her crutches out from the back. She carefully made her way up the steps and knocked. Selma opened the scarred, wooden door. She wore her usual work attire, cargo trousers and a T-shirt, with a tea towel slung over her shoulder.

"Tallulah, you made it."

"Good evening, Selma. Thank you for inviting me."

"Well, we can't have you wasting away while you're here. Dee would kill me. Come on in."

Selma stepped back from the threshold, making room for Tally to enter. The smell of roasting vegetables and chicken assailed her nose, and her stomach growled. Selma laughed, closing the door.

"Looks like the invite was well timed."

Tally blushed. "I guess noodles and soup aren't very filling."

"Dinner won't be long. Caitlyn is in the lounge. Go on in and visit while I finish up."

Tally nodded and began a slow trek through the kitchen, up the hallway, and into the living room. Her steps felt heavier than normal, her pulse hammering. She licked her lips, wishing she had thought to ask Selma for some water. As she entered the lounge, she saw Caitlyn sitting in an armchair. Her eyes were closed, her hands tapping to an imaginary beat. Her legs bounced sporadically. As if sensing Tally's presence, Caitlyn opened her eyes. She smiled widely, her jerky movements stilling.

"Hey, you made it."

"Yeah. I can't wait to eat. It smells heavenly in here."

"Mum has always been an excellent cook. It's a good job I work hard and swim a lot, otherwise, I'd be huge."

Tally came fully into the room and chose to sit on the other armchair adjacent to Caitlyn. She lowered herself with a groan, her muscles pulling. She had stayed in the shower longer than her body would have liked, and she was paying for it now.

"Are you okay?" Caitlyn asked.

"Funny, I was going to ask you the same thing." When Caitlyn raised her brows in question, Tally explained. "When I came in just now, you were fidgeting quite a lot."

"Oh, that's nothing." Caitlyn waved her off. "I told you, I'm a very restless person. Nighttime is the worst. I can manage a couple of hours, but then I'm up roaming the house and looking for something to do."

"Doesn't that bother you?"

Caitlyn shook her head and shrugged one shoulder. "I rarely take any notice anymore. It's just who I am."

Caitlyn's words seemed sincere enough, but Tally could see the slight dimming of her eyes. Years of police training had taught Tally how to read people, how to spot a lie, and it was clear to her that Caitlyn wasn't as fine with her troubles as she purported. She wanted to ask more questions but didn't want to upset Caitlyn, so she held her tongue. "I called my buddy earlier. He's going to look into that information you wanted."

Caitlyn's eyes dimmed even more, as she looked toward the kitchen. "That's great. Hopefully, I'll get some answers."

Tally reached over and covered Caitlyn's hand where it still rested on the arm of the chair. "I don't want to sound pessimistic, but don't get your hopes up too high. Selma could just as easily be telling the truth."

"You don't really believe that, do you?"

Tally glanced away. Her heart told her that Selma would never lie to Caitlyn, but her head said differently. It was just too strange of a thing for her mother not to tell her about Caitlyn's and Karl's accident. Or for Selma not to bring it up when she stayed twelve years ago. She looked back at Caitlyn and shook her head. "No, I don't. But I don't want you to be hurt by the truth. Isn't it better to not know?"

A flash of anger zipped across Caitlyn's features. "I hardly remember anything of my first twenty years on this planet. I deserve to know everything. Even if it hurts me. My brother died that day. I want to know what she's hiding."

"Okay, I'm sorry. I'm just concerned about you."

Caitlyn's face softened and she smiled. "It's okay. Thank you for caring. I'll be fine."

"Caitlyn?" Selma's voice sounded from the kitchen. "Set the table, please."

"Already have, Mum," Caitlyn called back. She rolled her eyes at Tally. "I set the damn thing an hour ago. She knows I do everything straight away. Idle hands and all that."

"Do you ever rest?"

Caitlyn grinned, then bit her lip and looked away, as if not wanting to say something. She glanced back at Tally. "Actually, I had quite the good nap earlier," she admitted.

Tally blushed as the memory of them curled up together on the sofa penetrated her mind. "I must have too, considering I didn't remember how we ended up like that."

"Despite your nightmare, it was very relaxing. I can't remember the last time I napped during the day. I'm always so filled with energy. I think…" Caitlyn stared at the wooden floorboards, her brows drawn down.

"What?"

Caitlyn gazed back up at Tally silently for a moment.

"What is it?

"It doesn't matter." Caitlyn rose from the chair and started to move away, but Tally grabbed her wrist and stopped her.

78

"Tell me." Tally's heart pounded painfully. Caitlyn's gaze roamed her face, from her eyes to her cheeks, to her lips, then back to her eyes. She looked petrified of something. "You can tell me, Cait," Tally whispered.

Caitlyn blew out a breath. "I don't know what it is, but for some reason, when I'm in your presence, the lightning in my body and brain vanishes." Caitlyn's pupils darkened, her voice almost a whisper. "Replaced with a calm I don't ever recall feeling, not even in the lake. Almost like I was lost at sea and being near you brings me back to shore."

"Cait—"

"Crazy, isn't it? We don't even know each other. I'm going to go help Mum dish up."

Caitlyn strode from the room without giving Tally a chance to reply. Tally slumped back into the cushioned chair, feeling like she had been punched in the chest. Those were the most beautiful words Tally had ever heard. Never in her life had she thought her mere presence could affect someone so much. The confusion and longing in Caitlyn's gaze weren't hard to miss. *What is happening between us? She's right, we don't know each other. But don't we?* Every conversation, every interaction was bringing them closer together. Tally was afraid of what that meant. *I need to keep my distance. I can't be falling for her. I just can't.* Tally resolved to get through dinner as quickly as possible, then escape to her cabin. She would need to avoid Caitlyn as much as possible. She needed time to figure out what was going on between them, and she couldn't do that with Caitlyn being close to her and saying such beautiful things.

†

Tally didn't get her wish of escaping early. Dinner was amazing, she even went back for seconds, but sitting across from Caitlyn the whole time was torture. Every time Tally glanced up, Caitlyn was staring at her, a pensive look on her face. Conversation was sparse. For Tally, it was not knowing what was happening between her and Caitlyn. She assumed the same for Caitlyn. Selma did a good job of filling in the silences, talking about improvements she had made over the years and stories of her days being friends with Danielle. There was no mention of Caitlyn's accident or Karl's death. Tally realised she didn't even know where Caitlyn's father was, or even if he was alive. She made a mental note to ask Caitlyn about that at some point.

Tally placed her knife and fork down and leaned back with a groan. "That was delicious, Selma. I haven't eaten that well in weeks."

Selma beamed. "You're welcome. Seems you have a similar appetite to Caitlyn."

Although her words were innocent, Tally couldn't stop her cheeks from warming at the thought of just how similar their appetites were.

"Do you cook like this every night?"

"It depends on the schedule. I do try and cook a decent meal as often as possible, but sometimes it's just so busy around here that I just don't have the time." Selma glanced at Caitlyn. "It would be nice if my daughter cooked occasionally."

Tally gazed over at Caitlyn, who sported a frown. "You don't like to cook?"

Caitlyn narrowed her eyes, staring down at her empty plate. "It's not that I don't like to. It's not safe."

Tally raised her eyebrows and glanced at Selma, whose features matched her daughter's. "What do you mean it's not safe?"

"I get distracted. I set fire to the oven once when I forgot to turn down the gas on the hob. If Mum hadn't walked in at that moment, the whole place could have gone up."

"Yes," Selma said. "That was a scary day. And do you see why I keep on at you to be careful?"

Caitlyn folded her arms across her chest, her head lowered. To Tally, it seemed Selma was telling her off like a naughty schoolchild. Considering Caitlyn was in her thirties, it was uncomfortable to watch. Tally thought Caitlyn quite capable of a lot of things. Never once had she thought Caitlyn needed watching. *Perhaps I don't know the full extent of her injuries. Then again, she has no trouble working and swimming in the lake. She's allowed to drive.* She glanced back to Selma. Something didn't sit right in her gut. *Why does Selma keep bringing up how accident-prone Caitlyn is?* Tally didn't like to see Caitlyn sitting there clearly upset and annoyed. She tried to lighten the mood.

"Well, if it makes you feel any better, I'm not exactly great in the kitchen, either. You've seen what I brought here to live on. Not the healthiest of foods." That earned a grateful smile from Caitlyn.

"Well," Selma said, a slight irritation in her voice. "Your predicament is a lot different to my daughter's. If she isn't careful, one of these days, she could seriously hurt herself. Or someone else."

Caitlyn stood forcibly from the table, toppling her chair. She glared at Selma. "What is your problem? Why are you always going on at me?"

"Caitlyn, calm down. We have a guest."

81

"I don't bloody care. You're always alluding to my clumsiness or forgetfulness. Why can't you just let it go? I travelled the Goddamn world for years, without incident. I'm not a child."

"You're acting like one now."

Caitlyn took a few deep breaths, her gaze boring into Selma's. Tally kept her head down, making herself as small as possible. She was glad Caitlyn was standing up for herself, but she didn't want to be a witness.

Caitlyn glanced at her. "I'm sorry if I ruined your evening, Tally. I'm going for a walk." She stormed away from the table. The back door slammed behind her, as she left the house.

"I apologise, Tally. My daughter can be somewhat hotheaded at times."

Tally wanted to dispute that claim. It was obvious Selma's constant belittling had set Caitlyn off. Tally didn't say anything. She was, after all, a guest. It wasn't her business how the relationship between mother and daughter played out. However, she was desperate to go after Caitlyn.

"It's okay, Selma. I guess I should be going anyway. Can I help with the dishes?"

Selma waved her off. "No, thank you. You're a guest and not well. You go on home and get some rest. I'll take care of this."

"Are you sure?"

"Yes, positive. Maybe we can try this again sometime when Caitlyn isn't acting up."

Tally nodded, not trusting herself to speak. If anyone had acted badly, it was Selma. She got to her feet and walked to the door, her hip tight from sitting up for the last hour. "Thank you again for dinner. It was delicious."

Selma smiled. "You're welcome."

Tally settled herself into the golf cart and made a slow journey up the track. She kept a look out for Caitlyn, straining her eyes through the night. A few minutes later, she rolled to a stop outside her cabin. She wasn't surprised to see Caitlyn there. What did surprise her was that Caitlyn was standing in the lake, the water up to her knees. The night was cold, no doubt the water would be freezing.

Tally switched off the cart and grabbed her crutches. Gingerly, she made her way over the pebbles and shale to the shoreline, ending up next to Caitlyn's trainers and socks. "Cait," she called, raising her voice over the rustling of leaves from the wind. Caitlyn didn't turn around. She stood stock still, arms by her sides with hands clenched. "Caitlyn, come on. It's freezing in there." Caitlyn's head shook imperceptibly. Tally took a breath. "If you don't come out of there now, I'll have to come in and get you." That did it. Caitlyn turned around, her face lit by moonlight. Even from a distance, Tally could see the tear stains on her cheeks. "Please come inside." Tally didn't wait for her reply. She awkwardly crossed the stones and up the cabin steps, confident Caitlyn would follow.

Once inside, Tally laid her crutches down by the sofa and lit the fire. She limped into the bathroom and grabbed a clean towel. She returned to find Caitlyn just inside the front door, arms wrapped around her waist. Her skin ghostly white.

"Come here." Tally held her hand out. Caitlyn looked at Tally's hand and took a few steps forward. Tally took her elbow and led her to the fire. "Sit." Caitlyn did. After grabbing the throw from the back of the couch, Tally lowered herself to the floor, trying not to grimace at the pain in her leg. She lifted Caitlyn's left foot into her lap and dried it and her leg off. She repeated this on the other side. She tossed the towel behind her, then passed the blanket to Caitlyn. "Wrap this around yourself." Caitlyn stared into the fire, making no signs she'd heard Tally. "Please." Caitlyn's shoulders sagged. She took the throw and wrapped herself in it. Tally rubbed Caitlyn's feet to help circulate the blood.

They stayed that way for several long minutes, before Tally asked, "Did that help? Standing in the water," she clarified.

Caitlyn nodded. "My mind was going crazy." Her voice came out in a whisper. "I don't get why she keeps treating me this way."

"Has it always been like this?"

Another nod. "Yeah. She flipped out when I said I was going travelling. She doesn't think I can cope on my own. Just because I can't remember stuff, doesn't make me an invalid. I practically rebuilt the wharf by myself. I'm not helpless."

"I know." Not once since Tally arrived did she ever think that of her. Caitlyn might get distracted a lot and had an endless supply of energy, but she was just as capable as anyone. Probably even more so than Tally.

"Usually, I roll my eyes at her and tell her I'm fine, but tonight…." She shook her head, her fringe bouncing over her forehead. "Tonight it was different."

"Why?"

Caitlyn looked at her for the first time since sitting by the fire, her gaze intense. The firelight flickered in her irises, bringing to mind the image of fireworks exploding at New Year. Tally swallowed hard, mesmerised by her gaze.

"You were there," Caitlyn whispered. "I don't want you thinking I'm stupid, or useless." She looked away. "I'm sorry. I sound ridiculous."

Tally tightened her hold on Caitlyn's feet. "I've never thought that. Not once." It was Tally's turn to look away for a second. "What you said earlier, before dinner, that was the most beautiful thing I'd ever heard." She let go of Caitlyn's feet and carefully manoeuvred herself next to her, taking a chance they shared the same feelings. There was a spark between them, one Tally wanted to set aflame. Her earlier doubts vanished, as she gazed into Caitlyn's eyes. She couldn't keep away from her even if she wanted to. She cupped Caitlyn's cheek, running her thumb gently over the warm skin below her eyelid. She felt Caitlyn's breath coat her face, as her own breathing increased. "I don't know what is happening here, and frankly, I'm confused. We've only just met, but Caitlyn, you do something to me. Something I can't explain. And I don't want to." Caitlyn's eyes teared. She lowered her head and relaxed it against Tally's shoulder. Tally held her close.

"When I stormed out earlier, all I wanted to do was run as far away from here as possible. Without meaning to, I found myself stood outside your cabin. I looked toward the lake, the pull to go swimming stronger than ever. As I stepped into the water, the cold didn't penetrate and stop my thoughts like it usually does. You asked me earlier if it helped standing in the water. It didn't. For the first time in years, the lake didn't heal me." Caitlyn lifted her head and rubbed the few tears on her cheek away. "I heard your cart pull up. My heart rate settled. Then I heard your voice and my thoughts instantly stopped. Sitting here with you, now, I feel normal. I feel like myself before the accident. It's strange, because I don't remember how I was back then, but I think it felt like this. No agony. No need to run away. My mind is clear. I realise now, when I stormed out, I was running to you."

"Caitlyn." Tally's pulse pounded in her ears. Her hands trembled. Caitlyn's lips were so close to her own. All she would have to do is dip her head a couple of inches and she would be kissing her.

"How is it possible that you have that kind of power over me?"

"I don't know, but I feel it too. Even when you knocked me over that first day, I went to sleep at the cabin thinking about you." Tally cupped her cheek again. "Your eyes pull me in, and that scares me." The connection she felt to Caitlyn was stronger than anything she had felt for anyone before. It wasn't altogether welcome, but she wouldn't run from it. She couldn't.

"I want you to kiss me." Caitlyn's gaze slid to Tally's lips.

Tally wanted that, too. She lowered her head and shifted onto her bad leg. Cramp gripped her, and she pulled back from Caitlyn, clutching her hip.

Caitlyn's face turned from sultry to concerned in a flash. "What is it?"

"My hip is cramping. I need to lie down."

Caitlyn moved and gently pushed at Tally's shoulder, helping her to lie back. "What can I do?"

"Nothing. I just need a minute." Tally moved her leg into different positions, trying to stretch out the cramp. Her pelvis throbbed. She realised she hadn't had a pain killer since that afternoon. She gasped at the spasm. She concentrated on flexing her leg and eventually the cramp eased, replaced with a dull ache. Tally gazed up at Caitlyn, who was kneeling next to her, her gaze panicked. "I'm okay now."

"No, you're not. You're sweating." Caitlyn ran gentle fingers through Tally's hair and held her hand with the other. "Should I call a doctor or something?"

"It's fine. It happens a lot if I stay sitting in one place for a long time."

Caitlyn frowned at her. "Perhaps Emma is right and there is something wrong." She glanced up at the clock. "It's a little late to be calling her. I'll ring her first thing in the morning and see if she can come out and see you."

"You don't need to do that. She'll be back in a couple of days, hopefully with an X-ray booked." Tally squeezed her hand. "Honestly, I'm fine now."

Caitlyn stared at her for a long moment before finally nodding. "I should get going and let you get some rest."

Tally saw the walls go up instantly. A few minutes ago, they admitted there was a connection between them and were about to kiss. Tally's injury had ruined the moment. She tried to sit up, but Caitlyn kept her down with her hand on her shoulder.

"Let me get you your meds. Give them a chance to work. I don't want you in pain when you try to stand."

Tally nodded but didn't say anything. The pain was there whether she was on her meds or not. Just with them, it wasn't as bad. She recognised that Caitlyn was distancing herself. Why, she didn't know. "They should be on the kitchen counter."

Caitlyn stood and went in search of the meds, coming back a moment later with two tablets and a glass of water. She handed the dose over to Tally. "Will you be okay getting up on your own, or should I stay and help?"

Tally wanted her to stay, and not just to help her up. She wanted to talk to her again, maybe make good on that kiss, but distance was in Caitlyn's eyes. Caitlyn's fingers tapped against her thighs, her eyes darting about the room. *So much for my presence settling the storm within her.* Tally knew she was being harsh. Whatever this was between them was hard for Caitlyn to process. She deserved time to figure it out. *Or maybe the fight with her mother put her on edge and she was just looking for comfort. Now the moment has gone, and she's not interested.*

"You can go. I'll be fine." Tally placed the glass onto the hearth and sat up fully. "Will you be okay getting back on your own?"

Caitlyn raised an eyebrow and smirked. "We're on private property that I've lived on for years. I know my way."

Tally looked away, feeling foolish for assuming Caitlyn needed help.

Caitlyn cupped her chin and tilted her head up. "But thank you for worrying about me."

"You're welcome."

Caitlyn dropped her hand and stepped back. "I'll be by in a couple of days to change the sheets and bring you clean towels. Don't forget any shopping you need, just ring the main house and we'll add it to the list."

And just like that, Caitlyn was back to being professional. Tally's heart deflated at the change.

"See you around."

Tally didn't get the chance to say goodbye, as Caitlyn practically fled the cabin. The pain meds were taking effect. If Tally wanted to make it to the bed, she needed to move soon. Instead, she picked up Caitlyn's discarded throw and wrapped it around herself and settled next to the fire. She knew she would regret the choice in the morning, but she wanted to stay in the memory of having her arms around Caitlyn, warmed by the flames and from the heat of Caitlyn's gaze.

†

Caitlyn stepped through the back door. Selma was wiping down the countertops. She looked up, lips pursed. Caitlyn toed off her trainers and kicked them to the side. "We need to talk, Mum."

Selma tossed the cloth into the sink and placed her hands on her hips. "You're right, we do. What was that scene all about? You embarrassed me in front of Tallulah."

"I embarrassed you?" Caitlyn glared at her, anger building up inside. "You were the one who brought up my forgetfulness, treating me like an invalid."

Selma glanced at the tile flooring, her shoulders dropping a few inches. "You're right, I did. I'm sorry." She stepped forward and took Caitlyn's hands in her own. "I can't help it. I just worry about you all the time."

"Well, you don't need to. I've survived this long. I'm not incapable of living my life."

"I know." Selma let go and went to the dining room. Caitlyn followed, and they sat next to each other at the table. "Caitlyn, you have to understand. Ever since you came out of the hospital, I'm constantly worried something is going to happen to you. Every morning you swim in the lake, I'm worried you'll drown. I hear you at night, pacing your bedroom, or watch you spend hours staring at the computer, working on things that don't need doing. I swear if I didn't make you finish your work around here on time, you'd stay out there all night. You're my world, Cait. I don't want to lose you, too."

Caitlyn took a breath, listening intently to Selma's words. She understood her concerns, but that didn't mean she had to put up with being treated like a child, especially in front of Tally. "I get that, I do. But Mum, you have to let go. If you keep acting this way, all you'll do is push me away. I don't want to leave; I love it here, but I'll end up not having a choice."

Caitlyn hadn't wanted to make that threat, but she also couldn't put up with being smothered. Seeing the sadness in Selma's eyes almost made her want to stop looking into the accident. If Caitlyn found out Selma had been lying all this time, then she would leave, even if Selma started to treat her more like an adult. Doubts were creeping in. She didn't want to second-guess her decision to find out the truth. What she told Tally still played in her mind. She had lost her childhood, her brother, her memories. She deserved to know what happened.

Selma nodded, frowning as she did so. "You're right," Selma said. "I'm sorry. I'll try to do better."

"Thank you." Caitlyn leaned over and hugged her, hoping against hope that her mother wasn't lying to her about this or the accident. She pulled back and glanced at a photo album at the end of the table that she hadn't noticed when they first sat down. "What's that out for?"

"I got it out earlier to show Tallulah photos of Danielle and you two as kids." She shrugged. "I didn't get a chance to show her. I think maybe I'll take it to her tomorrow."

Caitlyn's pulse picked up. Her hands went clammy, not at the thought of Tally seeing her baby photos, but at the inability to remember the events depicted in the album. It was the same every time Selma got the albums out. Caitlyn had a few scattered memories and the vague sense of how it felt back then but nothing concrete. Over the years, she had made peace with losing the beginnings of her life. She had made plenty of memories since the accident and didn't feel she was missing out on much. However, when the photos came out the melancholy would set in. Knowing she would regret probing the past, she asked, "Do you mind if I take it upstairs and look through it?"

Selma looked surprised but nodded. "Of course. Do you want me to look through them with you?"

Caitlyn stood and grabbed the book, cradling it to her chest. "No, it's okay. I just want a chance to hide the embarrassing ones from Tally." She smiled widely, hoping Selma wouldn't spot her lie. The truth was she wanted to try and feel connected to her past. A foolish dream of maybe triggering a memory. It had happened before, it might again.

Selma nodded. "Okay." She stood and kissed Caitlyn on the cheek. "I'm going to go take a bath and head to bed. I need to be up early. Fredrick and I need to load up the Jet Ski and take it to the mechanic."

"I'll see you tomorrow. Good night, Mum."

"Goodnight, Caitlyn. I really am sorry about tonight."

"It's fine."

Once up in her room, Caitlyn stripped off and slid into bed naked. She tucked the thick blankets around her legs. She doubted she'd be getting much sleep. Her mind was too keyed up to relax. The memory of Tally's hand on her cheek sent chills down her spine. She couldn't believe she had begged Tally to kiss her. She would have willingly lay down with her and made love. *Thank God she got a cramp.* Not that she wanted Tally in pain, but if it hadn't have happened, Caitlyn had no doubt they would be having sex by the fire. *And what a mess that would have been.* Caitlyn knew the attraction between them was strong, and she was terrified. She had never been so open with anyone before, not even Emma. She still couldn't believe how easily Tally settled every racing thought, every tick, everything that made Caitlyn who she had become. *She is like the frigid depths of the lake, stilling my frantic being into calm.* That was the thing that scared Caitlyn the most. She had never met anyone who could do that to her, and that's why she had fled. She'd run away from Tally's healing powers. She didn't know what it all meant, why it was Tally who could do that to her, but she was in no mood to figure it out.

Avoidance was key. She would ask Selma to do the towel and linen changes for her. That way, she wouldn't have to see Tally so soon. If she could avoid her for long enough, that might give her the chance to get her emotions under control and figure out what it all meant.

With that plan set in her mind, she reached over to her nightstand and lifted the photo album into her lap. This wasn't an album she remembered seeing before. Selma had so many of them; eventually they all blurred together.

Taking a deep breath, she opened the cover. The first photo she saw was of her and Karl dressed up for Halloween. She guessed she would have been about seven, Karl only a couple of years older. She recognised her mother in the background, dressed as a witch.

She flipped the page. Her father smiled up at the camera, cradling a newborn in the hospital. Caitlyn didn't know if that was Karl or herself in his arms. She hadn't seen her father in over ten years and had no clue where he lived. He had begun to distance himself from her after the accident. Selma said the grief of losing his son had weighed him down, and he couldn't cope with it all. He took to self-medicating with painkillers, even going as far as stealing Caitlyn's prescriptions. When Selma found out, that was the beginning of the end of his relationship with them. Caitlyn had no desire to find him.

The next few pages of photos were filled with snapshots over the years, none of which brought forth a memory for Caitlyn. Her foot began to wiggle up and down under the blankets. Her other knee bounced, causing the images in the album to jump around. Her movements stilled, as she turned another page. Her gaze landed on a photo of two toddlers. She recognised herself sitting on the left, dressed in a white dress embroidered with small daisies.

The girl next to her wore pale-blue dungarees with a cartoon dinosaur stitched on the chest. *Tally.* Tally's bright green eyes shone through the photo and pierced Caitlyn with their familiarity. Tally's little arm was wrapped around Caitlyn's waist, pulling her in close as she smiled for the photographer. Caitlyn wasn't looking at the camera. Her gaze was fixed on the dinosaur, her small fingers touching its head.

Caitlyn's vision blurred as tears filled her eyes. She reached out and traced the photo with trembling fingers. She wished with all her heart she could remember this moment. Even if she hadn't had the accident, she doubted she would remember this day. They couldn't have been more than three or four years old. *I wonder why Mum and Danielle drifted apart. They were such good friends back then. What could have happened that put such distance between them?* Caitlyn knew Selma had moved away after divorcing their father and buying the lake, but surely their friendship would have survived. *From the way Mum spoke about them growing up over the years, it's obvious they were best friends. I know she speaks to her once a year but why no more than that?* Selma held genuine affection for Tally, that was clear. Caitlyn couldn't think of a reason why Selma and Danielle still wouldn't be as close.

As Caitlyn continued to gaze at the photo, her mind drifted to what could have been if Tally and herself had grown up together. *Would we be best friends like Mum and Danielle? Or would we have developed the same attraction we have now?* She pulled the photo from under the plastic and tossed the album onto the floor, too distraught to continue going through it. She opened the drawer on her nightstand and placed the photo inside. She switched off the lamp and snuggled down into the sheets. Caitlyn closed her eyes and tried to shut her mind off to the multitude of thoughts swirling around.

An hour later she had done nothing but toss and turn and huff in annoyance. She flopped onto her back and peered up at the ceiling. Her fingers drummed on the mattress, her toes flexing in time. *This is useless.* Normally her restlessness didn't bother her. If her body needed sleep then she slept, eventually. *Tonight, I wish sleep would come.* The day had been long and emotional. All she wanted was a few hours of respite.

She closed her eyes again and cast her mind back to sitting by the fire with Tally beside her. She concentrated on the feel of Tally's arm around her, Tally's hand on her cheek. Caitlyn's breathing evened out and deepened. She thought of the photograph in her drawer, of how close they used to be. Before she knew it, her body had stilled. Her breathing lengthened, and she drifted off. Tally's face was the last image she saw.

CHAPTER EIGHT

Tally's eyes fluttered open, the chill of the room raising goosebumps on her skin. She pulled the throw tighter around her body. She had expected to wake up in pain, but there was none. For the first time in months, her pelvis and hip felt normal. She couldn't explain why that was, and she didn't care. All that mattered was waking up without discomfort. Considering she had slept on a hard floor all night, she had expected a lot worse.

She sat up and rubbed the sleep from her eyes. Carefully, she stretched her legs. She noticed only a slight twinge in her hip. *Maybe the wood flooring helped.* She took the chance of standing up, using the coffee table for balance, and put her full weight on her leg. It held up well. Not wanting to risk this good fortune, Tally picked up one of the crutches and used it to get herself to the bathroom. After taking care of her business she went in search of coffee.

The sun wasn't quite up yet. The cabin was still cast in shadows. Tally wrapped the throw around her shoulders and carried her coffee out onto the deck to watch the sunrise. She settled onto the lounge chair. The lake was eerily silent, only the occasional bird tweeting its presence. She should have been relaxed sitting in the quiet of the morning, but she was on edge. The evening's end kept replaying itself over in her mind. They had been so close to kissing that Tally could almost taste Caitlyn's lips. *If I hadn't gotten a cramp, would we be waking up together?* Probably, so it was a good thing her hip acted up. Tally hadn't even told Caitlyn how she got her injury. Jumping into bed with one another would have been a mistake. Tally resolved to get to know Caitlyn better. *Maybe I could invite her over for coffee or dinner.* Tally's doubts about pursuing things with Caitlyn were cast aside while they sat so close together by the fire. All she wanted was to see if their personalities would mesh as well as their physical chemistry so obviously did.

As the sun peeked up from the horizon, a familiar swim cap caught Tally's attention. She grinned, thanking the gods for sending Caitlyn her way so early. Talking to Caitlyn now wouldn't give Tally the chance to get overly nervous about speaking to her. If she had to wait all day, she had no doubt her anxiety would be through the roof.

She gulped her coffee, then hefted herself from the lounge chair. She made her way to the balustrade, watching Caitlyn's powerful arms pull her ever closer to shore. Tally smiled as Caitlyn's head rose from the water about halfway across the lake, pointing toward Tally's cabin. Tally lifted her arm to wave, but Caitlyn's head went back down, and she reversed her direction. Tally frowned, her brows pinched together, as Caitlyn swam away. It didn't take a genius to know Caitlyn had avoided doing her usual lap of the lake to evade Tally. *I guess she's still freaked out by last night.* Tally tried not to take it too personally, but it was hard. All she wanted to do was talk to her. It looked like she would have to wait for another day. *She's coming by tomorrow to change the sheets. I'll talk to her then.*

The following afternoon, Tally waited eagerly by the door when she heard Caitlyn's cart crunching over the gravel. Her stomach was in knots. She was so excited about finally seeing her again after nearly two days. She had tried to keep her mind off Caitlyn by doing her exercises and reading. Those activities hadn't helped. Her thoughts always returned to Caitlyn. She had been on the deck first thing in the morning again, waiting to see Caitlyn swim by. Caitlyn had either gone swimming even earlier or hadn't gone at all. Again, Tally tried not to take it personally. She could have tried to track her down, however, she knew Caitlyn needed time. Tally was content to wait for her.

And now she was here. The cart drew to a stop outside, and Tally pulled the door open. Her welcoming smile vanished, as she saw Selma climb from the cart.

"Good afternoon, Tallulah," Selma called, as she grabbed an armful of linens from the back of the cart.

"Hey. I thought this was Caitlyn's task?"

"Usually it is. She's gone into town to meet up with a friend."

Tally bit her lip, hoping Selma didn't see her disappointment. It was painfully obvious now that Caitlyn was avoiding her. Tally didn't know if it was because Caitlyn wasn't interested or if she feared being alone with her.

Whatever the reason, it was apparent Tally wouldn't be seeing her soon. *Maybe I should just pack up and go home. I came here to get better, not have my heart chasing a woman who wants nothing to do with me.*

Selma climbed the steps, her smile friendly. "Before I get started, I just wanted to apologise for the other night. I was out of line with Caitlyn, and I ruined the evening."

"Nonsense. It was a little uncomfortable, but it's fine. I had a nice time." *Especially after I came back to the cabin.* "You don't have to change the sheets for me. I can handle it myself."

"No, you won't. Dee would have my head if I didn't look after you properly."

Tally grinned. "Mum is a worrywart. I can cope with making the bed."

"But you don't have to." Selma smiled and entered the cabin.

Tally followed her in. "Can I get you a coffee or anything?"

"No, thank you. I must crack on. Work never stops around here."

Selma disappeared into the bedroom, while Tally sat at the breakfast bar. A few minutes later, Selma re-emerged, her arms now filled with Tally's old sheets and towels.

"Did Caitlyn bring you the photo album?"

"Sorry?"

"I dug out an old photo album to show you. There are some pictures in there from when you were kids."

"No, she didn't." *Hard to bring me something when she's avoiding me.*

Selma shook her head. "That bloody girl, always forgetting stuff. Tell you what, why don't you come to the main house Friday night, and I'll show it to you then. I'm doing a barbecue down by the jetty. You can get fed again, and I'll embarrass Caitlyn with her baby photos."

"I'm not sure if that's such a good idea." *I highly doubt Caitlyn would want me there.*

"Why not? It's not like you're busy up here."

"True." Tally had already read the three books she had brought with her. She had nothing else to do except download more or stream a film on her phone. She found herself agreeing to the invitation. Just because Caitlyn wanted to avoid her, that didn't mean Tally should give up the chance for some decent food. "Okay, I'll come. But don't forget I have a big appetite."

Selma let out a throaty laugh. "Oh, don't worry, there will be plenty for everyone."

Tally watched Selma pack the linens into the cart and set off down the track. She had two days before the barbecue. Two days of waiting. She hoped she would get to see Caitlyn before then, but she doubted her chances. Caitlyn had gone out of her way to avoid Tally, but Friday night she wouldn't succeed. Selma would make sure Caitlyn was there, of that Tally was sure.

†

Friday afternoon, Caitlyn stood at the main desk, checking on next week's bookings. The front doorbell jingled. She glanced up, ready to greet whoever it was, but her smile didn't come to her lips. Emma stood there, dressed in her usual cargo trousers and T-shirt. She looked as good as Caitlyn remembered, but the spark of attraction she once held for Emma was absent.

100

Emma grinned, ogling what she could see of Caitlyn over the desk. "What a lovely surprise."

"Hardly a surprise when you know I work here. I assume you're here to see Tally."

Emma nodded. "Yes. Selma said last time I could just drive on up, but I wanted to let you know I was here, so you didn't think a stranger was on the property."

That's a load of bullshit. We all recognise your damn Jeep. Caitlyn refrained from the snarky comment. "Very thoughtful of you."

"While we're chatting, how do you fancy coming out with me sometime? I feel like we have some unfinished business. I miss you."

Caitlyn licked her lips, her fingers drumming on the appointment book. Going out with Emma would be a big mistake. Not only was Caitlyn's mind filled with Tally, but being with Emma had brought her nothing but confusion. She couldn't imagine a life of running away from someone and the unsettling thoughts they inspired. *Being next to her is nothing compared to being with Tally. Tally is the one who stills my insides. I can't give that up.* Despite not seeing each other for a few days, Tally was still on her mind, *a lot.* Caitlyn wasn't sure what she was waiting for. Her heart recognised Tally as someone she could trust, but her head didn't want to play ball. She was struggling with the urge to just let go and see what would happen between them.

"I don't think that's a good idea, Emma."

"Why not? We were good together."

Caitlyn blew out a frustrated breath. "I explained why I left, but you didn't, or wouldn't understand."

"Then give me a chance to listen. Just one date."

"As I said—"

"Emma!" Selma came from nowhere and stepped up and hugged Emma. "It's great to see you again."

"You too, Selma. I was just catching up with Caitlyn."

Caitlyn kept quiet as the two talked back and forth. Selma had always liked Emma. Caitlyn did too. She was gorgeous, successful, and had a wicked sense of humour. If not for Caitlyn's apprehension of always being on edge around her, she probably would have still been with her. Selma hadn't understood why Caitlyn had broken up with someone so well suited to her. Caitlyn tried to explain, but her words never made sense to either of them. In the end, Caitlyn gave up trying to make them understand and just said it was over. Things had been fine, right up until Emma turned up as Tally's physiotherapist. Caitlyn was okay with Emma helping Tally. Tally deserved the best, and that was Emma. That didn't mean she liked seeing her. Tally was due to stay for the next few weeks. Caitlyn didn't think she'd be able to cope with seeing Emma all the time.

"Of course it's fine, isn't it Caitlyn?"

"What?" Caitlyn had zoned out and hadn't paid any attention to what they were talking about.

"I said, it's fine for Emma to come to the barbecue tonight."

Hell no! "Um."

Emma furrowed her brows as she studied Caitlyn. "Maybe I shouldn't, Selma."

"Nonsense. We've known you for years. All the guests are coming. It'll be great to catch up with you properly, won't it Caitlyn?"

All the guests? Does that mean Tally is coming? Caitlyn wanted to scream at the absurdity. The last thing in the world Caitlyn wanted to do was spend the evening with Emma and

Tally. She just knew Emma would spend the entire time trying to convince her to give their relationship another chance. And what would Tally do? Caitlyn didn't want Tally watching Emma trying to charm her. That would just be mean.

"I'll have to check it's okay with Tally," Emma said. "To make sure she won't mind seeing me outside of our professional relationship."

"I'm sure she'll be fine with it," Selma replied. "She's pretty laid back."

"Great. Well, I'll see you both later. I must crack on." Emma grinned at Caitlyn and left.

Caitlyn stared at the closed door. "What on earth are you doing, Mother?"

"Playing matchmaker, of course."

"I'm not interested in Emma. You know this."

"It doesn't hurt to at least try to be friends with her." Selma touched Caitlyn's arm, her gaze pleading. "You've known each other for years."

There was no point arguing with her. The invitation had already been extended. Emma was coming. All Caitlyn could do now was try to keep her distance and hope Emma got the message she wasn't interested. Her main concern was seeing Tally again. Caitlyn knew she had probably hurt Tally's feelings by staying away, but she hadn't had a choice. It was too confusing being in her presence. *Looks like I don't have a choice now. At least with Tally there, I won't be so overrun with my distractions.*

†

103

"You've improved your range of motion." Emma bent Tally's leg and pushed it toward her chest. "You've clearly been doing the exercises I set for you."

Tally smiled, even though her hip was aching. She relaxed her hands where they gripped the edge of the table she was lying on. "Yeah, I want to get better as soon as I can. And there's not much else to do around here anyway."

"Well, you've done brilliantly in just a few days." Emma stepped away and wrote some notes in Tally's file. "I still want you to have an X-ray, just to be sure. I've managed to get you an appointment for Monday morning at ten thirty. Will that be okay?"

Tally nodded despite not knowing how she'd get there. Caitlyn had offered to take her, but that was before she started avoiding her. Tally doubted she would still want to do it, so resigned herself to booking a taxi. "That's fine. As soon as we know everything is all right, I can begin doing more work."

"As I said, we can't rush the healing process. It could still be weeks before you're fully able to walk without assistance."

Tally remained positive, despite Emma's warning. The sooner she got better, the quicker she'd get her life back. *What life? The thought of going back to work terrifies me, and I live alone. I'm not exactly brimming with options.* She shook the maudlin moment away. Every night, she made up a bed on the hard floor, and every morning her pelvis and hip felt slightly better than the day before. She was positive the soft bed she had there and at home misaligned her joints and was causing the cramps and stiffness. Sleeping on the floorboards wasn't the comfiest she had ever been, but the benefits were outweighing the negatives.

Emma slipped the file back into her bag and helped Tally stand. "I won't be at the appointment, but I'll get a report sent to me. I'll come back here Wednesday, and we'll see where we are."

"Sounds good." Tally went to the kitchen and poured herself a glass of water. The effort to get through the physio had dehydrated her.

"Listen, there's something I need to talk to you about."

Tally raised her brows in question. "Okay."

"I'm sure you're aware by now that Caitlyn and I used to be close."

Tally kept silent, not wanting to comment just yet. She felt her pulse spike at the thought of where this could be going.

"I've known her and Selma for several years. Selma has invited me to the barbecue tonight."

"Oh." That'll be fun, watching Emma cosy up to Caitlyn.

"I agreed to come, but only if you're okay with seeing me in a social setting. I obviously won't be discussing anything about your treatment, but I would like a chance to reconnect with Caitlyn."

"You don't need to worry about that. I'm fine seeing you out and about. Besides, I doubt I'll be going myself anyway. I'm exhausted from the session. I'll probably just chill out and head to bed early." Tally was exhausted, but she had been excited at finally seeing Caitlyn after three days of avoidance. She had wanted a chance to talk to her, to get to know her. There was no way she would get the chance with Emma there. *Caitlyn is obviously okay with Emma going to the barbecue. Perhaps I've misread this whole situation, and Caitlyn isn't into me like I thought.*

"Oh, well I hope you do come. Selma's the best at barbecues, especially her corn on the cob."

"We'll see."

"Okay. If I don't see you later, I'll see you Wednesday. Keep up with the exercises."

Emma lifted her bag and table and left. Tally leaned against the countertop, hands balled into fists. "I guess that's that, then." She shook her head and carried her glass over to the couch. She made herself comfortable and switched on the television. She was in no mind to try and fight for something she didn't even know really existed. *The fact Caitlyn has stayed away from you should have clued you in. She isn't interested. At least you found out before you made an idiot out of yourself.*

†

The late afternoon turned into evening, and Tally must have dozed off. Someone knocking on the door startled her awake. She twisted her head and saw Caitlyn through the glass on the other side, wringing her hands together. Tally got to her feet and opened the door. "Hey."

"Hi. Can I come in for a minute?"

"Sure." Tally stepped back from the threshold and allowed Caitlyn to pass. "Shouldn't you be at the barbecue?"

Caitlyn glanced around, then settled her gaze on Tally. She nodded. "That's why I'm here. Mum sent me to find you. The food is almost ready."

"I'm not feeling up to it, sorry."

"Tally…"

"What?"

"I'm sorry I've been avoiding you." Caitlyn shrugged. She looked over Tally's shoulder, rather than facing her. "I got scared and confused."

"It doesn't matter. From what I hear, you're in good company at the barbecue."

Caitlyn's face flushed, but she didn't look away. "It's not what you think. Mum is quite taken with Emma. She invited her, and I didn't know how to say no."

"You don't have to explain anything to me." Tally hobbled over to the kitchen and pulled some juice from the fridge. She wasn't thirsty, but she needed something to distract herself from Caitlyn's wounded eyes. "Emma still likes you. You should give her a chance. You never know, she might be the one."

"I'm sick and tired of people telling me what I should and shouldn't do." Caitlyn's voice rose, her frustration apparent. "There are a million little reasons why I do not want to get back together with Emma, and one very big reason." Her direct stare bored into Tally's.

Tally's breathing increased from the intensity. She raised a brow, waiting for Caitlyn to continue.

"You, Tally. Even if I weren't attracted to you, I still wouldn't want to be with Emma."

"So, you do like me?"

Caitlyn came closer. The corners of her lips rose slightly. "I would have thought me asking you to kiss me the other night would have clued you in to that."

"But you went silent on me."

"I know, and for that I'm sorry. As I said, I was scared and confused. I'm not confused anymore. I'd very much like to get to know you better." Caitlyn glanced away for a second. "That's if I haven't ruined everything."

Tally swallowed hard. Her head told her it would be too much trouble getting into something with Caitlyn, but her heart begged her to take the chance. She found herself agreeing with her heart. "You haven't ruined anything. But next time, just talk to me."

Caitlyn nodded. "I will."

"Good." Tally smiled, her heart letting go of the heavy load it had carried for the last few days.

"So, will you come to the barbecue?"

"I can't. It would kill me to see Emma fawning all over you."

"I promise there is nothing between her and me."

"I believe you, but I can't make myself do it."

Caitlyn nodded again, then stepped around the counter and right up next to Tally. "I understand. I have the afternoon off tomorrow. Maybe we could do something then?"

Tally took a shuddering breath, having Caitlyn so close was playing haywire with her brain. "I'd like that. I'm not sure how far I'll get, but I'd love it if you showed me around the woods. I've been aching to go exploring again like I did the last time I was here."

"I'd love nothing better. There's a trail that loops around the property line and through the trees. It's flat enough for the cart to drive around it. We can take that. I'll even pack a picnic."

"What will you tell Selma?"

"That I'm showing you around. She won't think it's weird."

"Okay." Tally clasped Caitlyn's hands. "Until tomorrow then."

"Tomorrow." Before Tally had the chance to move, Caitlyn leaned up and kissed her cheek, stepping back before

Tally could do more. "I'll tell Mum you're sorry you couldn't make it tonight."

"Thank you."

"No problem. I'll see you tomorrow."

"Goodnight, Caitlyn."

Tally watched her leave, then leaned heavily against the counter. Her whole body seemed to let out a collective sigh. *We're back on track. God, I so wanted to kiss her right then.* She instantly regretted not agreeing to go to the barbecue, but her reasons were valid. As much as she wanted to spend the evening in Caitlyn's presence, there was no way she would enjoy herself with Emma there. *At least I'll get her all to myself tomorrow afternoon.*

She couldn't wait for tomorrow to arrive.

CHAPTER NINE

Tally watched the tree line. Caitlyn should be emerging any minute, ready for their afternoon together. Tally had been waiting for nearly half an hour. Her eagerness to see Caitlyn had her filled with an excitable energy. She had been dwelling on the fact Caitlyn had avoided her all week. In the back of her mind, she couldn't stop thinking about what might have happened at the barbecue between Caitlyn and Emma. Caitlyn saying she wasn't interested in Emma didn't stop Tally from wondering. The whir of the golf cart penetrated her fog of worry and brought back the excitement. Tally's smile grew, as the cart came into view. Caitlyn was behind the wheel. *Right on time.* Caitlyn rolled to a stop and grinned up at Tally.

"Hi," Caitlyn greeted.

"Good afternoon."

Caitlyn got out of the cart, dressed in comfortable shorts and a simple T-shirt. She wore a baseball cap, with the Leighton Lake logo embezzled on the front. Despite her casual attire, Tally thought she looked gorgeous.

"I thought maybe you might have changed your mind."

Caitlyn frowned and narrowed her eyes. "Why would I do that?"

Tally shrugged and looked away. "I thought maybe Emma—"

"Stop."

Caitlyn held her hand up, palm forward, and came up the steps. She stopped right in front of Tally and grasped her waist. Caitlyn leaned up and kissed her hard on the mouth. Caitlyn's lips were soft but demanding. Tally held herself back from deepening the kiss. Her mind buzzed, and tiny zaps of electricity shot through her body. All thoughts of Emma disappeared.

Caitlyn pulled away. "Does that help?"

Tally nodded. Her hands trembled where she tightly held her crutches. Her legs were weak before. After kissing Caitlyn, she was struggling to stay upright. "Yeah, that helped."

"Good. Before we go, you need to know, Emma did bring up us dating again. I told her no. I'm only interested in you, Tally."

Tally grinned. "You can keep reminding me by kissing me again."

Caitlyn playfully slapped Tally's stomach with the back of her hand. "All good things come to those who wait." Caitlyn stepped back and bounded down the steps. "Come on, let's get going."

Following at a steadier pace, Tally made her way down the steps and put her crutches in the back of the cart. She noticed two cool bags and a large blanket already nestled inside. She settled next to Caitlyn and placed her hand on Caitlyn's thigh. "Lead on."

Caitlyn turned the cart around and drove to the back of Tally's cabin and toward the woods, where the trail started. Before long, they were covered by the canopy of trees, the sunlight straining to breakthrough. Caitlyn took them deeper into the woods, before coming to a wire fence that stretched off into the distance. Tally spotted grazing cows and an old farmhouse up on a hill.

"You see the cow over there?" Caitlyn asked. "The one with a white head and the black patch on her hind?"

Tally followed Caitlyn's finger, as she pointed to the cow in question. "Yes."

"We call her Houdini. She's the one who keeps managing to make it onto our property. Fredrick spends most of his time fixing the fence. My idea was just to leave the fence open and let her come and go as she pleases. Mum wasn't happy about that suggestion." Caitlyn laughed. "I understand how Houdini feels, being trapped someplace you don't want to be."

Tally cut her gaze to Caitlyn. Although her words were said with a laugh, her eyes said something different. "Do you mean being here? At the lake."

Caitlyn's brow furrowed, as she looked off into the distance. "Sometimes, but mainly up here." She tapped the side of her head. "It's hard not being able to switch off from your thoughts, especially when they all jumble together." She glanced at Tally. "That's why I was so surprised I managed to fall asleep with you on the sofa. That's never happened before. Anyway, sometimes I feel like Houdini, and I just want to escape from my body. That's why I like swimming in the coldness of the lake. It's like it freezes my insides. For the hour I'm in there, I feel almost normal." She glanced at Tally again. "Just like being with you, except I'm not cold with you, I'm hot." Caitlyn pulled away and carried on their journey.

Tally cleared her throat, amazed at how open Caitlyn was. "Are you always so honest?"

"Mum will tell you, I speak before I think. It does get me in trouble at times."

"I can imagine."

A few minutes later, Caitlyn switched off the cart. "This'll be a good place to stop."

Tally looked around. She'd been so caught up in watching Caitlyn, she hadn't noticed the passing of their surroundings. She also hadn't noticed the incline, so slight as it was. They had stopped on a hill overlooking the lake. A few trees still surrounded them, but it was easy to spot the main house in the distance.

"It's beautiful up here." When Tally came to the lake with her friends, she never took the time to immerse herself in her surroundings. They were all too busy goofing around on the lake and drinking beer. Gazing out over Leighton Lake beyond the canopy of trees was breathtaking. She turned to Caitlyn. "How far are we from the cabin?"

"We're about three-quarters of a mile from the main house. Your cabin is over there." Caitlyn pointed to the left.

Tally dipped her head in different directions, trying to spot her temporary home through the woods. She could just make out the chimney.

"It's pretty flat here now," Caitlyn said. "If we walk a few minutes this way, there is a nice spot to have the picnic."

"Sure." Tally got out of the cart and retrieved her crutches, while Caitlyn grabbed the bags and blankets. "I'm sorry I can't help carry anything."

Caitlyn waved her off. "It's fine, it's not that heavy. Besides, if you fall over carrying this, I doubt I'd be able to pick you up."

Tally's gaze roamed Caitlyn's body, grinning as she did so. "I don't know, you look pretty strong to me. And don't forget, you've helped me up plenty of times before."

"True, but I'd rather not repeat it."

Tally would gladly fall over if it meant having Caitlyn's hands on her again. She refrained from making that wish aloud. Carefully, she followed Caitlyn through the remainder of the trees. She concentrated on not tripping over any tree roots or divots in the earth. After a while of traversing the uneven ground, the hard mud gave way to long grass. Tally looked up, seeing a large open field, bordered on the other side by more trees. She followed Caitlyn for another minute, then stopped in a small patch where the grass was flattened. She glanced at Caitlyn, who was spreading the blanket out. "It's a bit odd finding this flat bit amongst the long grass."

Caitlyn's neck flushed. "I come up here a lot on my time off, when I want to get away from everything." She knelt on the blanket and began unpacking items from the bags. "It's not as calming as the lake, but it's a good second choice. When I'm here, I let my thoughts run wild. I don't try to control them."

Tally dumped her crutches down and lowered herself onto the blanket, stretching her bad leg out in front of her. "Cait?"

Caitlyn looked up but didn't stop her unpacking. "Yeah?"

"I'm sorry things are difficult for you. And before you say it's fine and that you're used to it, I know it hurts you. For that, I truly am sorry."

Caitlyn nodded but didn't speak. She lowered her head and finished laying out the items. She passed Tally a paper plate. "Help yourself."

Tally scanned the offerings. It was clear Selma had cooked way too much at the barbecue. The blanket was filled with sausages, burgers, rolls, and veggies. "You can't beat leftovers." Tally loaded her plate and dug in.

"Can I ask you something?" Caitlyn asked a few minutes later.

"Sure."

"Do you remember me as a kid? By the way, I was meant to bring you a photo album of Mum's. That was difficult to do, considering I was avoiding you at the time."

Tally laughed. "Yeah, that wasn't a fun few days."

"Sorry."

"It's okay, we worked it out. Continue."

"Well, I found a photo in there of us as toddlers. It didn't ring any bells to me. I wondered if you had any memories of us back then?"

Tally looked skyward. She studied the few clouds that floated across the sky. "Kind of." She looked back at Caitlyn. "I remember Mum taking me to her friend's house a lot and playing with her kids. I vaguely remember you and Karl. I do remember we stopped going when I was about six or seven. You would have been the same age. After that, I only remember Selma coming to visit, and soon that stopped, too."

"Why do you think our mums stopped being so close?"

Tally shrugged. "I don't know. I never took any notice growing up. I was too busy with school and my friends. I know they talk at Christmas and send the occasional letter. I just assumed they drifted apart."

"I guess."

"What is it?"

Caitlyn blew out a breath and put her hotdog down. She folded her hands in her lap. "I don't know. I just have this feeling it's tied into my accident."

"But they stopped being friendly long before then."

"I know. I just feel like something happened back then, and it's part of the reason why no one told you about Karl dying, or my head injury."

"I still haven't heard from my buddy. I'll give it a couple more days before I call him again."

Caitlyn smiled. "Thanks. It'll be nice to know the truth, whatever it is. Anyway, how's the food?"

"It's great. Makes me sorry I missed last night."

Caitlyn winced. "Actually, I'm glad you weren't there."

"Why?" Tally knew it had something to do with Emma, and she was positive she would regret asking.

"I was in the kitchen tidying up when Emma got ready to leave. She cornered me. After pleading again for another chance, she kissed me."

Yep, shouldn't have asked. Tally briefly closed her eyes to stop her jealousy from rising. Caitlyn had already made it clear it was Tally she was interested in, but that didn't stop her from being hurt.

"I pushed her away and demanded she leave. I think she got the message I wasn't interested, but she'll probably keep trying."

"I'm going to find another physio."

"You don't need to do that."

"I do. And not only because seeing her here upsets you. I'm not sure I can have her working with me knowing she kissed you. That's my job."

Caitlyn's eyes widened at Tally's fierce tone. Her features relaxed as she grinned. "Is it now?"

Tally's gaze bored into Caitlyn's. "Yes."

Caitlyn got to her knees and crawled over to Tally. She placed a hand on her shoulder, her head inches from Tally's. "You may regret taking up that position."

"Really?" Tally's breathing increased. The scent of Caitlyn was turning her insides to liquid. "Why is that?"

"I work my employees hard."

"Bring it."

Caitlyn lowered her head and captured Tally's lips in a ferocious kiss. Tally ran her hands up Caitlyn's arms and into her hair, knocking her ball cap off in the process. Before she knew it, Tally was falling back onto the blanket with Caitlyn on top of her. The kiss turned hungry. Caitlyn's hands roamed over Tally's face and neck. Tally cupped Caitlyn's butt and pulled her closer. It was getting out of hand, but Tally didn't care. All she wanted was to have Caitlyn surrounding her, inside and out. The world fell away, leaving only the two of them. Caitlyn's hand drifted down Tally's side toward the drawstring on her jogging bottoms. The thrill of knowing where Caitlyn intended to be caused Tally to flinch her pelvis upwards, the movement jarring her hip. She wrenched away from Caitlyn, pushing her off, as pain shot down her leg.

"Mother fucker!" Tally ground out.

"I'm so sorry." Caitlyn's voice was panicked, as she sprang off Tally.

Tally opened her eyes, her breathing laboured, not just from the pain, but from Caitlyn's kisses. She reached out and took Caitlyn's hand. "It wasn't you. I promise."

Caitlyn squeezed her hand and ran her free hand through Tally's hair. "Are you okay?"

"Yeah, I just need a minute." Caitlyn attempted to withdraw, but Tally held her hand firmly. "Lie with me."

"Are you sure?"

"Yes."

Caitlyn's smile was magnetic. She pushed the containers of food to one side and settled down next to Tally's good side. They lay together, with Caitlyn's head resting on Tally's chest, and Tally's arm wrapped around Caitlyn's shoulders. "This is nice."

"Better than nice." Tally kissed the top of Caitlyn's head. The enjoyed the silence for a few moments.

"Will you tell me what happened?" Caitlyn asked.

Tally didn't need to clarify what Caitlyn was referring to. She swallowed hard, recalling the night she was injured. Even thinking about it brought her out in a cold sweat. With Caitlyn lying next to her, she felt safe relaying the awful event. She closed her eyes against the bright blue sky, pulled Caitlyn tight against her, and readied herself to talk.

CHAPTER TEN

Caitlyn could feel Tally's heartbeat thump in her chest beneath her head. She could also feel the tension in Tally's body. Tally said she was willing to talk about what happened to her, but as of yet, she hadn't spoken. Caitlyn regretted asking, stirring what were obviously painful memories for Tally. She lifted her head and gazed down at Tally, whose eyes were screwed shut. Tally's breath came in quick gasps.

"Hey." Caitlyn reached up and cupped Tally's cool cheek. When her eyes fluttered open, the anguish they revealed nearly broke Caitlyn's heart. "It's okay. You don't have to tell me."

Tally gave a small smile and pushed her cheek harder into Caitlyn's palm. "I'm all right. It's just hard to talk about."

"You don't have to. I can see this is difficult."

"I want to. You told me about your accident. It's only fair I reciprocate."

Caitlyn shook her head, her fringe falling into her eyes. "It isn't a competition."

"I know, but I want you to know me, all of me."

Caitlyn gazed into Tally's eyes for a moment, then nodded. "Okay." She rested her head back onto Tally's chest and waited. She didn't care if it took all night for Tally to open up. She'd gladly wait forever if it made Tally more comfortable. She didn't have to wait much longer. Tally's voice was quiet, as she started to speak. Caitlyn kept a firm arm around Tally's waist, hoping it helped to keep her safe and grounded.

"I told you about Ryan, my partner on the force. We were on the night shift. It was a Sunday night and quiet, for the most part. We patrolled around the city centre and nearby neighbourhoods, stopped for coffee, and responded to the occasional call. Everything was standard.

"About one in the morning, we were dispatched to a domestic disturbance. The details were sketchy. A neighbour had called in, saying she heard shouting and screaming coming from next door. She was worried about the woman who lived there. We just assumed it was a case of alcohol intoxication causing a row between husband and wife.

"We arrived and approached the door. We could hear them shouting. The woman was pleading with whomever it was to leave. He was screaming at her that he wasn't going anywhere. Ryan knocked on the door and announced our presence. The shouting stopped. A moment later, the door flew open. This huge hulk of a man stood before us in nothing but jogging bottoms. His body was covered in sweat.

His eyes were massive, nothing but pupil. It was clear he was more than just drunk." Tally paused for a moment. "I pulled my taser from my waistband, and was about to order him onto the ground, when he bolted toward us. He knocked Ryan off his feet and blew past me. I gave chase. The guy jumped into his car. I went to the passenger side, Ryan to the driver's side, and we fought to get him out of the car. I was half in, half out when the guy slung the car in reverse. I lost my footing and went under the front wheel."

"Oh, God." Caitlyn lifted her head, her heartbeat thundering. Tally's face was pale. A sheen of sweat beaded on her forehead. "That's horrible."

Tally blew out a breath, her whole body trembling. "I wasn't hurt badly right then. My thigh burned, but I was able to get to my feet. I wasn't quick enough to get out of the way, though." Tally's voice grew softer. "He gunned the engine and headed straight for me. He smashed into my side, and I went up onto the bonnet and over the top. All I remember is my body exploding in pain. I hit the ground with such force, I punctured a lung. I couldn't feel my legs. I thought I was going to die."

Caitlyn felt tears running down her cheeks as she listened. She pressed her lips together to stop herself from breaking down completely. She knew Tally had been injured on the job, but she didn't think for one moment it was as bad as this. "You must have been so scared."

Tally nodded, her own tears slipping from her eyes. "The pain was excruciating. Ryan's face came into view. He looked terrified, but he made all the right calls to the emergency services. I could hardly breathe and knew I was slipping away. I blacked out and woke up in the hospital two days later."

"Did they catch the guy?"

"Yeah. About a mile up the road. He'd lost control of the car and wrapped it around a tree. Walked away without a scratch. I had a body cam on, so he couldn't deny what happened. He's on remand now and should be sentenced in a couple of months for the assault on me and for beating his girlfriend."

"Do you need to be there?"

Tally shrugged. "If I want to be. I've been asked to make an impact statement."

"Will you go?"

"I'm not sure yet." Tally took a deep breath and smiled. "Anyway, I'm sort of glad it happened."

Caitlyn raised her eyebrows, shocked Tally would ever say such a thing. "How can you say that?"

"It led me here to you."

Caitlyn relaxed her features and kissed Tally on the cheek. "That's sweet of you to say, but I'd rather this hadn't happened to you." She lightly ran her hand through Tally's hair. "I'd prefer it if you found your way here another way."

"I guess. I *am* glad I'm here, though."

"Me too." Caitlyn kissed her on the lips, this time lacking the passion from earlier. As much as she wanted to, this wasn't the time to allow their desire for each other to take over. Now was about showing Tally how deeply Caitlyn cared for her. "How long were you in the hospital?"

"A few weeks. I was doing all right at home. Mum and Dad helped out a lot. Ryan stayed with me for a while. And there was Annabelle."

"Who's she?"

"My ex. At the time she was my live-in girlfriend, until it got too much for her and she left one day out of the blue."

Caitlyn sat up; incredulous Tally's girlfriend had left like that. "She left because you were injured?"

"I don't know exactly why she left. She didn't say goodbye, and I haven't spoken to her since. I think she couldn't cope looking after an invalid."

"That's a load of bullshit. You don't turn your back on someone you're in love with."

"Then I guess she wasn't really in love with me."

"Is it wrong that I want to kick her ass for doing that to you?"

Tally grinned and sat up, flipping her hair back from her face. "No, it's sweet." She leaned forward and kissed Caitlyn. "Thank you for sticking up for me."

"Always." Caitlyn did some quick calculations in her head. By her reckoning, Tally had only been single for a couple of months. The fear of being a rebound bubbled through her gut. "How long were you two together?"

"About three years."

Caitlyn looked away, brushing her hand through her hair. *That's a long time.* "So, you've only been single a few weeks?"

"Yeah, about two months."

"Right." Caitlyn continued to stare off into the distance. *How gutting is it that the one person I feel totally relaxed around is probably on the rebound? This sucks.*

Tally's hand cupped her jaw, turning Caitlyn's head to face her. "I know what you're thinking. You're not a rebound. If I'm honest, things with Annabelle had been stale for a long time. We were making plans, but neither one of us was totally into it. My accident just brought our break-up around quicker."

"How can you be sure? Yeah, we get along great, but we've only known each other a few days."

Tally took a breath and focused her gaze intensely on Caitlyn. "You're not the only one who feels a connection between us. From the moment I met you, I haven't been able to stop thinking about you. I know in here"—she tapped her chest—"that this is real. Please, believe me."

Caitlyn stared at Tally for a long while. Slowly her doubts drifted away. Her connection to Tally was stronger than she'd had with anyone. That kind of feeling had to mean more than just the physical. Caitlyn nodded. "I believe you."

Tally smiled and kissed her cheek.

"Thank you for telling me what happened. I know how difficult that was for you."

"Yeah it was, but I feel lighter for talking about it."

Caitlyn held Tally's hand, entwining their fingers. "How do you fancy going back to the cart and finishing the trail?"

"I'd rather stay here holding you."

"Such a charmer."

Tally shrugged a shoulder. "Just the truth."

Caitlyn kissed her quickly, and they settled back down onto the blanket. Caitlyn peered up into the sky. With Tally's arm around her, Caitlyn's whole body relaxed. This was different than the other times she had been near Tally. Everything inside her felt at peace. She had no thoughts, no restless energy, just a sense of tranquillity she never wanted to let go of. *I'm falling in love with her. I know I am. What will I do when she has to leave in a few weeks?* She released the thought from her mind and just immersed herself in the present. She was determined to enjoy being with Tally, no matter how short a time that would be.

Tomorrow could wait.

†

Caitlyn rolled the cart to a stop and switched off the battery. The sun had begun its descent, and the cool breeze that came with evening chilled her skin. They had been on the hill for nearly three hours, talking and getting to know each other. Caitlyn had talked of her time travelling, and Tally regaled her with some of the more amusing call-outs she'd had on the job. Caitlyn hadn't wanted the nice afternoon to end.

"I had a great time," Tally said.

Caitlyn smiled. "Me too."

"Do you want to come inside for a coffee or something?"

"As much as I would love to, I need to go check in with Mum."

Tally's eyes dimmed. "Okay."

"I'll take a rain check though."

"Great." Tally quickly kissed Caitlyn on the lips and extricated herself from the cart, grabbing her crutches from the back. "Come by anytime."

"I will. Oh, Tally?"

"Yeah?"

"I was thinking, maybe you should keep seeing Emma."

Tally furrowed her brow. "Why?"

Caitlyn blew out a long breath. "She is the best at what she does. I'll just make sure I'm not around when she visits."

"I don't think that's a good idea."

"Please, Tally. You need to get better, and she can get you there quickly. Look at how much progress you've made so far."

Tally frowned but nodded. "I definitely have improved tenfold since she started to work with me, and it's only been

125

two sessions. She's even got me the X-ray booked for Monday morning."

"See? She's the best thing for you right now."

"You're the best thing for me." She grinned and waggled her eyebrows.

"Funny." Caitlyn shook her head at Tally's teasing. "What time is the appointment? I'll take the morning off and give you a lift."

"You don't have to do that."

"I said I would. What time?"

"Ten thirty."

Caitlyn nodded. "Okay. We will need to leave about nine forty-five."

"Will I see you before then?"

"I'll be in the lake first thing tomorrow morning. Maybe I'll swim by and say hello if you're awake."

"Oh, I'll be up and waiting."

"Have a nice evening, Tally."

"See you later."

Caitlyn switched the cart back on and headed back to the main house, a smile on her lips. It had been a great day. As much as she wanted to go inside with Tally and continue into the night, she knew they needed to take things slowly. The attraction was already moving at lightspeed between them. Caitlyn didn't want to make a mistake and jump too far ahead when they were still getting to know each other properly. *If her X-rays are good, maybe I'll talk her into swimming with me next week.* The image of Tally in a swimsuit made the rest of the journey back home pleasantly uncomfortable.

She pulled the cart into the shed, grabbed the bags and blanket from the back, and bounded toward the main house.

Selma was sitting on the back porch, a bottle of Coke in hand, gazing out over the lake. She turned her head as Caitlyn approached.

"Hello, Caitlyn. Did you guys have a nice time?"

Caitlyn took a seat next to Selma, a smile playing on her lips. "Yeah, it was good. We followed the Bracken Wood Trail."

"Is Houdini still on the right property?"

"She was when we passed." Caitlyn chuckled. "I'm not sure how long that will last."

"I might have to think about putting more than just wire around the border."

"That'll cost a fortune."

"I know, but I can't keep having her approach the cabins. She about gave poor Mrs. Jenkins in Cabin Three a heart attack the other day."

"Well, so far she hasn't moo-ved."

Selma rolled her eyes at Caitlyn's joke. "How was Tally on the trail? I hope you didn't make her walk too far."

"She's all good." *Really good.* Caitlyn's lips still tingled from Tally's kisses. "She has an appointment Monday morning at the hospital. I said I'd take her. If you want, while she's there, I can pop into the shops and do the grocery run instead of on Tuesday."

"That'll be fine. We have a new arrival Tuesday morning, so it would be good to get their essentials in."

Caitlyn shook her head. "Why is it we still don't have a proper schedule for checking in and out?" It made sense to Caitlyn to have specific time slots. That way they weren't all over the place with guests coming and going.

"I like the guests to have the freedom they want. It doesn't bother me if it takes them all day to check out."

127

"Yeah, but then we scramble around trying to get the cabins cleaned and ready for the next arrivals."

"And that is why I never book someone in on the same day as guests are leaving."

"It still seems strange to me."

Selma tutted as she shook her head. "It's worked this way since I've had the place. I don't see a problem with it."

"I'm never going to change your mind, am I?"

"You can keep trying, but I don't see the point. Anyway, Emma called for you when you were out. She wants you to call her back."

That'll be never. "Okay."

Selma narrowed her eyes. "I don't believe you."

"I don't see the point of calling her back. I'm not interested in her anymore." *Especially after she tried to force her tongue down my throat.* Caitlyn had been too stunned to push her off right away. It didn't take long to come to her senses and shove her off. She couldn't believe Emma had done that. She was even more shocked she had the nerve to call. Caitlyn would need to have a serious talk with her and make her understand there was no chance of them reconciling. *Not tonight, though.* She didn't want to ruin her good mood by speaking with Emma. "I just wish she'd leave me alone."

Selma took a sip of her Coke. "Okay. It's clear you don't want to date her. I'll stop with the matchmaking."

"I'd appreciate that." Caitlyn stood and picked up the cool bags and blankets. "I'm going to sort this lot out and have a shower."

"I'll see you for supper."

"Yep."

Caitlyn went inside and unloaded the bags. All the while, her thoughts remained on Tally. They had come so close to making love out in the field. Having Emma work with Tally wasn't ideal, but she could get Tally better quicker. The sooner Tally healed, the sooner Caitlyn might be able to have her wish fulfilled and get her hands on Tally's naked form.

CHAPTER ELEVEN

"Ryan, are you sure?" Tally lowered herself onto the sofa and propped her leg up on the cushion.

"Yes. There was no reported accident along that stretch of motorway for the entire day. I did a deeper search and found it happened on the M5, just past Bristol."

Tally took a breath, her thoughts whirling. Selma had been truthful about Karl racing another car and the tyre blowing out, but the motorway it happened on was miles away from where she told Caitlyn. She couldn't figure out the need to lie. *Karl and Caitlyn weren't going to see their father in London as reported. But where?* "Thanks, Ry. I'll let my friend know."

"You're welcome. How's the healing going?"

130

"Better than I hoped." She didn't yet know the outcome of the X-ray from the day before, but she could feel in herself that everything was fine. She knew the reason she hadn't gotten better sooner was her lack of trying back home. Being truthful, she hadn't had the motivation back then to get better. She had been too distraught from the accident and with Annabelle leaving. Feeling sorry for herself hadn't helped. Out here, with the fresh air and meeting Caitlyn, her motivation had come back. She wasn't looking forward to seeing Emma tomorrow, especially after Emma had kissed Caitlyn. But Caitlyn was right; Emma was the best at her job. "I only use one crutch now, and that's only just in case. I'm walking around the cabin unaided."

"That's awesome, Tally. I can't wait to get my partner back."

"Me too." Tally put as much enthusiasm into her reply as she could, but she wasn't sure she even wanted to go back.

"I gotta run. My shift starts soon."

"Okay, I'll see you later."

Tally tossed the phone onto the cushion next to her and ran her fingers through her hair. She hadn't seen Caitlyn since Monday morning, and the wait was killing her. She hadn't been up early enough that morning to catch her in the lake and assumed Caitlyn had been too busy working for the rest of today to pop by. Tally glanced at the clock. It was nearing dinner time, and the thought struck her to invite Caitlyn over. She picked up her phone and called the main house. After a few rings, the line was picked up.

"Leighton Lake, how may I help you?"

Blood rushed to Tally's ears at hearing Caitlyn's voice. She grinned, remembering their time on the hill. "Hey. It's Tallulah Roberts from Cabin Seven."

"Oh, hello. How may I help you this evening?" Caitlyn's tone was playful.

"I was just wondering if the policy at Leighton Lake is still to give the guests what they need for a comfortable stay."

"It most certainly is. What may I assist you with?"

A night of passion would be my idea. "I was hoping, if you're free tonight, you might come to dinner at my cabin. Maybe help start a fire and snuggle in front of it."

"Well, that's not usually within the parameters of our services, but for you, I'm sure I can make an exception."

"That's great. I've missed you."

Caitlyn laughed. "It's only been a day."

"That's too long."

"I've missed you too, but it's been crazy busy here today. Spending the evening with you would be a welcome relief."

Tally thought of one way she could relieve Caitlyn but refrained from saying it out loud. "Come on by whenever you're ready. I'll be waiting."

"I'll look forward to it. Oh, Tally, do you have anything decent there to eat?"

Tally frowned, thinking about the noodles and soup in her cupboards. "Yes?"

"Hmm, why do I get the impression that your idea of decent is rather different than mine? Don't worry about it. I'll rummage something up from here."

"Are you sure? I feel bad for inviting you for dinner and not having anything to serve you."

"It's fine. Besides, I'm sure I'll find something to satiate my appetite."

Tally's stomach did a low roll, her clit twitching at the sexy quality of Caitlyn's voice. She swallowed hard. "I'm sure you will."

"I'll be about an hour. Is that okay?"

"Hurry."

Caitlyn's laughed flowed down the line as she hung up. Tally tossed the phone down again and rose from the couch. She had an hour to get ready. Despite her leg feeling good, it still took her longer than normal to shower. Plus, she wanted to shave her legs, just in case.

As she set about getting ready for the shower, her mind went back to the phone call with Ryan. She would need to tell Caitlyn about the call. She just hoped Caitlyn wouldn't get too upset about Selma's lie. There was a good chance Selma remembered the wrong thing about the road they were on, but Tally wasn't sure that was the case. Caitlyn had been right, Selma was hiding something. Tally wished she could call her own mother and ask about the discrepancy. With Danielle being on the cruise, she wouldn't be able to reach her easily. It didn't help that Danielle didn't own a mobile phone. Tally had no idea why her mother refused to get with the times. Danielle always insisted that if someone needed her, they could use a landline. Tally often thought it was just because Danielle didn't like trying to learn how to use technology. She could find out the cruise ship information from Jimmy, but she didn't want to involve him in all this. No, Tally would talk to Caitlyn first and see what she wanted to do about it.

†

Tally had just settled a blanket in front of the fire when a knock came at the door. She glanced up and saw Caitlyn on the other side, a smile on her face and a picnic basket cradled in her arms. Tally smiled back and went to let her in. She pushed the door wide and stepped aside.

"As promised." Caitlyn stepped through the doorway and handed over the basket.

"Thanks." Tally took the hamper and placed it on the floor by her feet. Her stomach clenched with nerves. It had only been a day since she saw her last, but she was unsure how to welcome Caitlyn. She wanted to kiss her but didn't know if Caitlyn would want that. They may have shared a few steamy kisses on the hillside, but that didn't mean Caitlyn wanted them now. Tally stuffed her hands into her pockets to stop herself from reaching out. "And thanks for coming over."

Caitlyn quirked an eyebrow. "You sound like I've come to fix a leaky tap, not have a date."

"A date?"

"Well yeah. That is what this is, right?" Caitlyn glanced around the living room.

The sun had set. The only illumination in the room came from the candles Tally had found in the store cupboard, creating an orange glow about the place. She had also piled up pillows and blankets on the floor, making a sort of nest for them to relax in. The whole scene was romantic. Anyone with eyes would see this as a date.

Tally nodded quickly. "Yes, it is."

"Then welcome me properly."

Tally grinned and stepped forward, taking her hands out of her pockets. She ran her fingers up Caitlyn's arm and cupped her cheek. "Welcome." She dipped her head and pressed her lips to Caitlyn's. Caitlyn grasped Tally's waist and leaned into her, bringing their fronts together. Tally groaned into Caitlyn's mouth and deepened the kiss, trailing her tongue over Caitlyn's lips and then crashing her mouth harder to hers.

After a few moments, Caitlyn pulled back but didn't loosen her hold on Tally. "Hi," she whispered.

"Hi," Tally replied, her breath coming quickly. Kissing Caitlyn was an experience she never wanted to stop having, both scary and exhilarating. She had no doubt their lovemaking would be just as intense. "I've missed you."

"Me too." Caitlyn leaned up and kissed Tally's cheek. "It feels like weeks since I saw you last."

"For me too. I tried to catch you in the lake this morning, but you weren't there when I got up."

Caitlyn stepped away and retrieved the basket, then carried it over to the blankets. "I didn't go out this morning." She knelt by the fireplace and began stacking logs and kindling into the fire.

Tally followed her over and lowered herself against the pillows. "How come?" Tally watched Caitlyn efficiently light the fire, her movements fluid and practiced.

"I didn't feel the need to go." Caitlyn added another log, then settled next to Tally, close but not touching. "There's only been a handful of times that's happened. Usually when I'm sick or something."

"What was different about today?"

Caitlyn shrugged a shoulder, her gaze penetrating as she stared into Tally's eyes. "Being with you has changed a lot of things within me. I know we haven't known each other long, but after being with you on the hill, that restless energy in me isn't there anymore. It's like you've healed something in me."

"Cait." Tally took Caitlyn's hand and entwined their fingers. Caitlyn had an amazing way with words. The love shining from Caitlyn's eyes warmed Tally's skin. It was clear they were heading toward something serious. Tally thought she would be scared, but she wasn't. Despite not knowing each other well, Tally knew in her heart Caitlyn was special. She so very much wanted to go on this journey with her. "You say the most beautiful things."

"It's all true." Caitlyn cupped Tally's cheek. "I could fall in love with you."

Tally took a breath and looked away. If she weren't careful, she would be begging to have Caitlyn naked in front of the fire. As much as she wanted to do just that, she knew her leg would get in the way and she wouldn't be able to do all the things she wanted to do with her. She tugged Caitlyn's hand to pull her closer and wrapped an arm around her shoulder. Caitlyn settled her arm over Tally's waist, her head tucked under her chin.

"Do you think this is crazy?" Tally asked.

"Probably. But I don't care. I love being here with you like this."

Tally kissed the top of Caitlyn's head. "Does Selma know you're here?"

"Yes. I've brought the photo album for you to look at. It's in the basket with some leftover casserole and rolls. Mum made sure to pack plenty, as she knows you don't eat properly down here."

"That's sweet of her." Talking about Selma brought to mind the other reason Tally had wanted to see Caitlyn. She didn't want to bring it up now and ruin the romantic atmosphere they were in, but she also didn't want to wait. Caitlyn had been wanting the truth for so long now that it wasn't fair to make her wait for the only bit of new information to come to light in the last fourteen years. "Talking of Selma, Ryan called me not long ago." Caitlyn stiffened in her arms but didn't move away. "He checked the information you gave me, and he couldn't find anything happening on the road Selma said the accident occurred on. After a little digging, he found the real location. It happened on the M5." This time, Caitlyn did pull away. Her eyes narrowed.

"What are you telling me, Tally?"

Tally took a deep breath, hating to have to be the one to break this news to Caitlyn. "According to Ryan, Karl did try and race a car and your tyre blew out, but it didn't happen where Selma said it did. She may have just been mistaken."

Caitlyn shook her head, her gaze going to the fire. She was silent for a moment before looking back at Tally. "That's not a detail you would get wrong. She told me Karl and I were on the way to see my dad, but the motorway you're on about is miles away from the direction to his. We were going somewhere different, but where?"

Caitlyn surprised Tally by cuddling up to her in their previous position. Tally had expected her to run and find Selma and demand answers right away. Tally kept silent, waiting patiently for Caitlyn to direct what would happen next. She didn't have to wait long. Caitlyn stood and grabbed the basket.

"I don't know about you," Caitlyn said, "but I'm hungry."

Caitlyn carried the basket to the kitchen, switched on the light, and set about warming up the casserole. Tally remained where she was, knowing Caitlyn needed to be doing something with the space to think. She could see the tremors in Caitlyn's body; foot tapping as she buttered the rolls, worrying her lip with her teeth. This was the Caitlyn Tally first met. She wanted to help her through this but didn't know how. She sighed, frustrated at her lack of action. She got to her feet and did the only thing she thought would help. She went to Caitlyn, turned her around, and wrapped her in a tight hug. Caitlyn resisted at first, but soon her head relaxed against Tally's chest. Tally relaxed, too, when she felt Cailyn's arms wrap around her waist.

"I'm sorry," Tally murmured.

"It's okay." Caitlyn's voice was muffled as she spoke into Tally's T-shirt. "I knew she was lying about the accident. I just hoped I was wrong." She lifted her head, tears in her eyes. "I'll need to talk to her, but not tonight. Tonight, I want to be with you and forget about all this for a while."

Tally nodded slightly. "Whatever you need."

"Thank you."

CHAPTER TWELVE

"Here you go." Caitlyn passed over the photo album. "There are a few of you in there, but it's mostly pictures of me and Karl." She crossed her legs and looked over into Tally's lap, as Tally began flipping pages. Dinner had been a quiet affair. After the hug in the kitchen, Caitlyn finished warming the casserole and they ate at the table in silence. She was thankful Tally was with her, but also allowing her the quiet time to think. Not that it did much good. Without her memories, there was no way she would be able to figure out what happened the day of the accident. She would need to confront her mother, she just didn't know how. *And what would be the point anyway? She'll only lie to me again.* Selma was more than likely to say she got the wrong road and had no idea where they were going. *Maybe it's time I just let it go. Unless I suddenly get my memory back, I'll never know the whole truth.* Caitlyn wasn't sure she would be able to do that, but she was determined to, at least, enjoy the rest of the evening with Tally.

"This one is cute."

Caitlyn looked up to see Tally tracing her fingertip over the very photo Caitlyn had removed from the album. She had replaced it just before packing up the picnic basket. She wasn't sure why, maybe to see if Tally got the same reaction she had. "Yes, it's one of my favourites."

"I look like a dork in those dungarees."

"I think you look sweet." She glanced up at Tally. "You still do."

Tally smiled, her cheeks tinting pink. "We seem to have been quite good friends as toddlers. I vaguely remember you back then. It was so long ago."

"Yeah. I guess, sometimes, pictures are all we have."

Tally covered Caitlyn's hand and squeezed her fingers lightly. "I think it's like that for most people's childhood memories, but at least I have some recollection. It must be so hard for you not to have anything."

"It's difficult to explain how it feels. When I try and recall the events before the accident, there's nothing there. I remember the photographs I've seen, but they aren't true memories." Caitlyn turned the album to get a better look at one of the pictures. "Some memories have come back, but I never know if I can trust them or if they are figments of my imagination. Sometimes, when I think of the photos, I feel like it's a memory, but again, I don't know for sure." She sighed and gazed into the dwindling fire. "That's why I went travelling. I wanted to make as many new memories as I possibly could, to help fill the void. It's not as frustrating as it first was when I came out of the hospital. I've learned this is who I am, and those parts of my life are gone for good."

"It's a good thing Selma took so many photographs of you all growing up."

"Yes. Without them, I'd have nothing."

Tally kissed the back of Caitlyn's hand. "You're a remarkable woman, Cait. You should be proud of yourself."

"Thank you."

Tally refocused on the album. "Oh my God, I remember this day."

Caitlyn looked at the photo Tally was grinning at. It was a funny scene. Both were sitting in a muddy puddle, grime covering their clothes. Caitlyn was crying in the picture, and Tally was hugging her. It was nice to look at, but it brought no recognition to Caitlyn. "Tell me about it."

Tally grinned at her. "Are you sure you want to know? You might not like me after I tell you."

Caitlyn narrowed her eyes and had a feeling she knew exactly why she was sitting in a puddle. "I don't need my memory to figure out it was probably your fault I'm crying."

"It was an accident, I swear." Tally grinned wider, her eyes dancing with mischief.

"Tell me," Caitlyn growled.

"We were running around outside, jumping in the puddles. It had rained heavily that day and we begged our parents if we could go play outside. I asked if you had ever eaten a mud pie." Tally fell silent, biting her lip.

Caitlyn glared at her, knowing what was coming next. "You pushed me."

Tally nodded, the corners of her mouth twitching as she tried not to laugh. "I didn't know you'd fall head first into the mud. You sat there with wet sludge sliding off your face.

I felt so bad that I sat in the puddle with you and hugged you. Selma must have heard you crying and, after seeing the state we were in, got her camera."

"I can't believe you pushed me!"

"I'm sorry. I swear, I never meant to make you cry."

"You know, I might believe you if you weren't sat here laughing your ass off." Caitlyn folded her arms across her chest in mock anger and stuck out her bottom lip in a pout. It was hard to be mad at Tally, especially as it was nice to hear Tally's memory of the event. She would treasure that gift for always.

"You can get me back if you like."

"I might just dump you in the lake."

"And I would deserve it."

Caitlyn looked at the photo again. It really was a funny picture. She slipped her finger under the plastic protector and pulled it out. "I'm going to frame this one and have it mounted on your wall at home to always remind you of how mean you were to me."

"It won't work. It'll always remind me of the night we sat in front of the fire, just the two of us."

Caitlyn sighed and rolled her eyes. "Now you've gone and ruined my revenge plan by being all romantic."

"Get used to it." Tally's gaze dropped to Caitlyn's lips. "I think that's enough picture time for now." She set the album aside and ran her hand up Caitlyn's thigh. "I want to kiss you."

"I don't think you deserve one."

Tally leaned in and trailed her lips over Caitlyn's neck. Caitlyn trembled at the softness of the kisses. She cupped the back of Tally's head, holding her closer. "That won't work."

"Really?" Tally moved to Caitlyn's earlobe, sucking gently. "How about now?"

"Hmm, my resolve is weakening."

Tally pressed into her, causing Caitlyn to fall into the blankets, her head sinking into a pillow. Tally stretched out on top of her, holding herself up on her hands so their bodies were not quite touching. She feathered light kisses over Caitlyn's face, staying clear of her mouth.

"Is your leg okay?"

"What leg?"

Caitlyn laughed and gripped Tally's waist, pulling her full weight on top of her. "Kiss me before you cramp up." Tally grinned, then captured Caitlyn's lips in a hungry kiss. Caitlyn could taste the casserole on her breath, mixed with Tally's unique flavour. She groaned as Tally pushed harder into her.

After a few moments, Tally released Caitlyn's mouth. "I want to make love with you, but I'm not sure if I'm up to the gymnastics."

Caitlyn smiled and kissed her again. Pulling back, she said, "I want that too, but I'm happy to wait." At Tally's pout, she clarified, "Well, not happy, per se, but I understand wanting to be fit and healthy. Once I get you into bed, I don't plan on letting you out for days."

"Days, huh?"

"Maybe weeks."

Tally kissed her quickly and rolled off, her breathing laboured. "In which case, we need to slow down."

Caitlyn tossed her thigh over Tally's good side. She snuggled in, with her arm over Tally's stomach and head on her shoulder. "You get me so worked up, Tally. My insides are screaming for you."

"I'm not very comfortable myself."

"Should I go? I don't want this to get out of hand. We're both on the verge of giving in." Caitlyn didn't want to leave, but it would lessen the sexual tension. *Maybe then I could relieve myself in bed.*

"Actually, I'd like it if you stayed. We can keep talking, we just need to keep our hands to ourselves."

"That'll be difficult." As if to prove her point, Caitlyn trailed her hand over Tally's belly and cupped her breast.

Tally covered Caitlyn's hand but didn't move it away. "Behave."

"You're making it difficult, because you're so sexy." Caitlyn lifted her head and gazed at Tally. "Talk to me about something boring, something that will douse the flames I have burning for you."

Tally was silent for a moment, then grinned. "Do you know there is a toad that gives birth out of its back?"

"That did it." Caitlyn extricated herself from Tally and sat up, brushing her fingers through her hair. "That's gross. Don't ever say that again."

"It's cute. All these little babies shooting out, leaping into the air."

Caitlyn covered Tally's mouth with her hand. "Stop. I'll throw up otherwise." She felt Tally's tongue swipe her palm. "Eww. That's even worse."

Tally raised her eyebrows. "I just had my tongue smooshing with yours, and you find that gross?"

"That's different. We weren't talking about toads then."

"You're so weird."

"And you like to torment me. Remind me again why I like you?"

"Cos I'm sexy." Tally smirked.

"Yes, you are. I need to freshen up." Caitlyn got to her feet and went to the bathroom, not surprised to find herself extremely aroused, despite the talk of toads giving birth. She thought about getting herself off quickly, but she knew it wouldn't be enough. Only Tally would be able to bring her the satisfaction she needed.

After finishing in the bathroom, she returned to the lounge. Tally had moved to the couch. "Everything okay?"

"Yeah, I just think it would be safer if we were up here and not on the floor."

"Good idea." Caitlyn settled next to Tally and snuggled up to her. "Shall we watch something on TV?"

"If you like." Tally reached over to the end table and grabbed the remote. "I wonder if there are any toad documentaries on."

Caitlyn laughed and playfully slapped Tally's belly, hoping she was joking.

†

Caitlyn pulled up outside the main house, noticing an unfamiliar car parked next to her mother's. She shrugged, assuming it was a guest, and got out of her car. She retrieved her suitcase from the back and headed toward the front door. It was ten at night. After driving for the last few hours, she couldn't wait to lie down in bed and sleep. Selma wasn't expecting her until the morning, but Caitlyn didn't see the point in staying in halls the extra night. She was desperate to get home and spend the next two weeks relaxing before heading back to university.

She opened the door. Voices wafted from the kitchen. She recognized her mother's but not the other person's. Selma's words stopped Caitlyn in her tracks.

"We agreed it was for the best. This hasn't been easy for me, watching you live your life with him."

"I know, and I'm sorry, but I can't leave my family."

Caitlyn crept closer, as she listened to the other woman's response, her stomach churning.

"Then why did you come here? You're just making it worse."

Caitlyn peered around the corner and saw Selma standing close to the other woman, whom Caitlyn vaguely remembered from her childhood.

"Even after all this time, you won't let me go." Selma seemed to be staring into the woman's eyes, unaware Caitlyn was watching. "You said you don't want to be with me, yet here you are."

"I just needed to see you. I miss you, Sel. These past ten years haven't been the same without you in my life."

Caitlyn inhaled sharply when the woman moved closer to Selma and kissed her quickly on the lips.

Selma pushed her away. "You can't keep doing this to me, Dee. It's not fair."

Caitlyn bolted awake. Her wide eyes frantically scanned the cabin, seeing nothing. Her heart pounded and blood rushed to her ears. *That can't be true. It just can't.* She got off the couch and paced the lounge, her brain struggling to make sense of her dream. She knew, without a doubt, that the dream was a memory. Tally's mother had kissed hers. *I feel sick.*

"Cait? What's wrong?"

Tally was still lying on the couch. They had fallen asleep together after watching a movie. They had both been so relaxed that Caitlyn hadn't wanted to go home. Tally pulled the throw off the back of the cushions and wrapped them up in it. Sleep came quickly for Caitlyn, quicker than ever before. She reasoned that was why the memory came back. Her brain had been rested enough to allow the memory to surface.

Tally sat upright and ran her hand through her hair. "Cait, talk to me?"

"I remembered something, something bad." She wasn't so concerned that her mother possibly had a relationship with a woman; that would be hypocritical. But the other woman was Danielle, the mother of the person Caitlyn was falling in love with. She also had a bad feeling this memory was connected to her accident.

Tally leaned over and switched the lamp on, her gaze concerned. She held out her hand toward Caitlyn. "Come sit, tell me about it."

Caitlyn stepped back away from Tally's outstretched hand. She couldn't be close to her and still be able to tell her what she remembered. She wrapped her arms around herself in a desperate attempt at comfort. She looked away from Tally's hurt expression. "I don't know where to start."

"Caitlyn, you can tell me anything."

Caitlyn looked again, seeing nothing but understanding in Tally's eyes. She lowered her arms to her sides and took a breath. "When I was nineteen, I came home from university early. When I got inside the house, I could hear Mum talking to a woman. The words between them were intimate. I eavesdropped. It was clear there was some kind of relationship between them. I peeked around the corner and saw the woman kiss my mum."

Tally blinked a few times. "Are you saying your mother had a lesbian affair?"

"I think so. But that's not what's bothering me." She looked away again, finding it hard to choose the right words.

Tally rose from the couch and approached Caitlyn. Her eyes were clouded with worry. She reached out and took Caitlyn's hand. "What is it, Cait? You're scaring me."

Caitlyn took a breath and held tighter to Tally's hand, using Tally's strength as an anchor. "It was your mother."

"What was?"

"The woman who kissed my mum."

Tally dropped Caitlyn's hand and stepped back. Her forehead creased as her brows pinched tightly together. "That can't be right." Tally shook her head. "It was just a dream, Cait. There is no way my mum would do that."

Caitlyn blinked and moved away. "I know the difference between reality and a dream."

"You said yourself, earlier, that sometimes it's hard to distinguish between your real memories and ones conjured through photographs."

"I know what I saw!" Caitlyn stomped back to Tally, her pulse hammering. "Your mum kissed my mum. There was something between them, and that's why they stopped being so close when we were growing up."

Tally puffed out a breath of air and sat back on the couch. She lowered her head and rested it in her hands. She didn't speak. Eventually, she looked up at Caitlyn, her expression pained. "I don't know what to believe. Mum and Dad have always been happy. I don't recall one argument between them. I just can't see her having an affair. A lesbian one at that."

Caitlyn stayed standing, staring into Tally's eyes. She found it hard to believe it herself, but she knew she was right. She wished she could remember what happened after that. *It's time to confront Mum.*

Caitlyn's gut told her that witnessing that kiss was the catalyst leading to her accident. She glanced at the clock. It was nearing one in the morning. Her mother would be in bed, but this couldn't wait. "I'm going to go wake up Mum. I need the truth."

Tally glared at her for a long moment, her features stoic, before finally nodding. "You're right. We can't go on not knowing what happened. Too many things aren't adding up."

"Will you come with me?"

Tally nodded again, then stood. "Of course." She stepped around Caitlyn and grabbed the crutch leaning up against the fireplace. "Are you sure you're ready to hear whatever she has to say?"

"Yes. It's time. What about you? This now involves your mother."

Tally sighed. "I'm not going to judge her for falling for Selma. Whatever happened between them isn't my business." She lifted her hand and cupped Caitlyn's cheek. "My only concern is for you. If my mum somehow was involved in your accident, I'll be less forgiving."

Caitlyn half smiled, pleased for Tally's support. "We'll get through this, won't we?"

"Are you asking if I still want to be with you?"

Caitlyn nodded.

Tally dipped her head and kissed Caitlyn gently on the lips. "Yes."

"Okay." Caitlyn had been worried that Tally might pull away. Their relationship had just been complicated by their mothers' apparent affair. Caitlyn didn't want that revelation to ruin her future with Tally. She was elated Tally hadn't pulled away from her. *Not yet anyway. We still need to find out exactly what happened back then.* Caitlyn took a deep breath, allowing the air to lessen her anxiety. She reached for Tally's hand. "Let's get this over with."

CHAPTER THIRTEEN

Caitlyn paced the kitchen. Tally sat at the small dinette table, her gaze tracking the frenetic movement. Caitlyn had woken Selma, and they were waiting for her to come downstairs. Tally's stomach felt heavy. She struggled to believe her mother had an affair with Selma. She didn't doubt Caitlyn believed what she saw but was sure Caitlyn had misremembered things from back then. It just didn't seem right that her mother had a relationship with Selma. Sure they used to be close friends, but an affair? *No, Caitlyn must be mistaken. As soon as Selma comes down, we can put this mess behind us.*

"Stop looking at me like that." Caitlyn stopped her pacing and scowled at Tally.

"Like what?"

151

"Like I'm confused or something. I know what I saw. You said yourself, things aren't adding up."

Tally looked away for a moment. "I just find it hard to believe it happened."

"It did happen. I know it."

"Okay, okay. I believe you." Caitlyn looked so fierce in her convictions that Tally's resolve melted. She still had her doubts, but she would wait until they heard Selma's side before passing judgment.

The sound of Selma's footsteps echoed through the hallway, coming closer. She appeared around the corner, tightening her robe. "What's going on? What's happened?" Her hair was mussed from sleep, and her eyes were slightly puffy. *She must have been in a deep sleep when Caitlyn woke her.*

"I need to talk to you, Mum. It's important."

Selma drew her brows down. "Can't it wait until tomorrow? It's the middle of the night."

"No, it can't. I remembered something."

"Oh, Caitlyn, that's great." Selma rushed over and took Caitlyn's hands in her own. Her face lit up with delight. "What was it?"

"I saw Danielle kiss you."

"What?" Selma's hands dropped to her sides, as she took a step back.

"The night I came back from university, you were in the kitchen talking with Dee. She kissed you. You told her how hard it was watching her live her life with Tally's dad."

"Caitlyn, this isn't funny." Selma glanced at Tally and straightened her posture. "You're wrong."

"I know what I saw. Stop lying to me."

"I'm not."

"Then how do you explain telling me Karl and I were on the way to see Dad when we crashed, when in fact, we were on a completely different motorway."

"What are you talking about?"

"Tally asked her friend on the force to find out if the accident happened the way you said it did. We were heading in the opposite direction."

"I must have been mistaken."

"Stop lying," Caitlyn shouted, causing Selma and Tally to flinch.

Selma looked at Tally again. "I can't believe you've gone along with Caitlyn's flights of fancy."

"I wasn't sure at first if what she thought was true," Tally said. She studied Selma's posture, her hand tapping her hip, the slight twitch of her lips. All her police training kicked in. Selma was hiding something. Tally glanced at Caitlyn and nodded, telling her she believed her fully. "But after we talked about it, nothing you said made sense. It wasn't logical that Mum never mentioned Karl dying or Caitlyn's head trauma to me. There was more to the story." She took a breath. "It's time for the truth, Selma."

Caitlyn reached out and touched her mother's forearm. "Mum, I'm not mad at you. I just need to know the truth. I deserve to know what happened back then."

"I need a drink." Selma went to the pantry and pulled out a bottle of rum. She retrieved a glass and poured herself a generous amount. After taking a long swallow, she sat at the table, cradling the glass in both hands. "I'm not sure what dragging all this up will achieve."

"I've been living in the darkness for fourteen years." Caitlyn sat next to Tally, opposite Selma. "It's time."

"All right." Selma took another quick sip. "I met Dee in our twenties. At the time, she was already dating Herbert, Tally's father. We became best friends. I eventually started to date Herbert's friend, your father." She looked at Caitlyn. "Over the years, my feelings for Dee became clouded. I found myself thinking about her all the time and wanting to spend time with her. Even after we both got married and had you girls, I still couldn't get her out of my mind. I was falling in love with her.

"Things with your father became strained. He noticed my feelings for Dee and eventually we split up. I was a mess. Dee comforted me, which only made my feelings for her stronger. I kissed her one night and confessed my feelings. She rejected my advances. Feeling alone, I bought the place down here, hoping to rebuild my life with you and Karl. I couldn't keep away from Dee, though. She felt the same. We had been best friends for so long, and we both wanted that friendship back. Gradually, we became close again. I would visit her as often as I could, and she would bring Tally and Jimmy down here with Herbert." Selma lowered her head, staring at the tabletop. She took a breath, her hands tightening on the glass. "I'm not sure how it happened, but Dee's feelings for me began to grow. She loved me back, but still loved Herbert. We kissed a few times, but never more than that. It got too hard for us both. I knew she would never leave Herbert, and I couldn't stand being on the sideline."

Tally's stomach sank further. It was all true. Her mother had been in love with Selma. To say she was stunned would be an understatement. She cast her mind back but still couldn't remember a time her mother was never completely in love with her father. *Perhaps Selma was right, and Mum just couldn't decide between them both. How hard that must have been for her back then.* "So that's why you stopped being friends?"

"Yes. Our connection was too strong though. We couldn't not be in each other's lives, so we stayed in touch a couple of times a year." Selma took Caitlyn's hand over the table. "That changed when you were nineteen. She came down to see me. Told me she wanted to see more of me, that she loved me. I told her I wouldn't have an affair with her. It wasn't enough. That must have been when you saw her kiss me. I said that I would always love her, and I'd be here if she ever got the courage to make the choice. She left not long after."

"I can't believe she loved you like that." Tally's whisper was barely audible. "She's never once given me the impression she wasn't happy with Dad."

"That's because she was, is, happy with him. That's why she could never choose between us. I think she loved us both equally."

"I'm sorry, Selma."

"It's okay, Tallulah." Selma smiled sadly. "I've learned to live with it. What I can't live with is what happened to Caitlyn."

"What happened, Mum, the day of the accident?"

"About two weeks after you saw us kiss, you and Karl confronted me. I guess you told him what happened, and you both wanted answers. I wasn't willing to talk about it. Karl said if I didn't tell you, he'd find someone who would. You ran out after him and you both sped off in his car. I could only surmise you were going to find Dee. I knew, for certain, when the police called and told me where the accident occurred. I rushed to the hospital. Karl was already gone. You were close to dying yourself. I was devastated that my feelings for Dee had caused the accident. If I had just talked to you both about it all, you never would have driven off."

"So you never told Mum about what happened?" Tally asked, incredulous that Selma wouldn't tell the woman she loved the most horrific thing that happened in her life.

"No, I did tell her. But I made her promise never to tell you."

"Why? What difference would it have made?"

"I was right, Tally," Caitlyn pulled her hand away from Selma.

Tally shifted, so she could see Caitlyn better. "About what?"

"Remember? I told you she didn't want you to know, because she was scared I'd find out the truth about the accident. I was right. She was covering her tracks. She never wanted me to know she's the reason my brother is dead and why I've lost half my life."

"It wasn't like that," Selma pleaded, her eyes filling with tears.

"Sure it was. You must have been elated when I woke up from my coma and couldn't remember anything."

"Caitlyn, no."

"It's true. And that's why you keep on about me being forgetful and not safe on my own. You were trying to get me to question my sanity. If I ever did remember, you could pass it off as my mind playing tricks." Caitlyn shook her head. "I can't believe this."

"Caitlyn, I swear it wasn't like that."

"I need to leave." Caitlyn's chair crashed against the wall as she stood. "I can't stay here a minute longer."

"You can't leave. Where will you go?"

"Anywhere, as long as it's away from you." She glared at Selma, then turned to Tally. "Tally, you coming?"

"What?"

"I'm leaving. You can stay here if you want, but I won't be around. I feel sick from all this." Caitlyn stormed from the kitchen and out the back door.

"Caitlyn, wait," Tally called, but Caitlyn was already gone. She glanced back at Selma, who sat staring after Caitlyn. She looked heartbroken at that moment. Tally was desperate to comfort her, but her heart begged her to go after Caitlyn. Caitlyn needed her more.

"It's okay, Tally. Go, make sure she's okay."

"Will you be all right?"

Selma nodded. "I'll be fine."

Tally got to her feet and grabbed her crutch. She didn't use it as she rushed after Caitlyn. She didn't care her hip twinged with every step. Caitlyn was storming up the driveway toward the exit. Tally quickened her step. "Caitlyn, stop!" Caitlyn slowed but kept walking. Tally caught up with her and grabbed her hand. "Where are you going to go?"

"Anywhere away from here."

Tally tugged her hand, forcing her to stop. "You can't just keep walking."

Caitlyn faced Tally, tear tracks visible on her cheeks. "Take me home, to your place."

"That's a three-hour drive away."

"I don't care."

"I can't just leave. Emma is coming tomorrow for my physio."

"You're right." Caitlyn pinched the bridge of her nose and then stared up at the night sky. "Your healing is important. I'll go find a hotel or something." She began to walk again.

"Cait! Please don't go." Tally's leg was throbbing. As much as she wanted to go after Caitlyn, there was no way she could keep going.

Caitlyn spun around. "I can't stay here, Tally. Not right now." She slowly walked back to Tally. "She lied to me for fourteen years. Karl is gone because of her actions."

"She didn't know it would turn out that way."

"God, I know that." She threw her hands in the air. "But she made it worse by lying to me. I have to leave."

Tally gazed at her for a moment, unsure of the right thing to do. Her heart told her to be wherever Caitlyn was. If that meant cancelling her appointment with Emma and driving through the night to get home, she would. She knew the best thing would be to stay and talk things through with Selma, but she also knew Caitlyn was resolute in her decision to leave. There was no choice to make. "Can you give me a few minutes to pack?"

"You want to come with me?"

"I never want to be without you." Tally closed the distance between them and wrapped Caitlyn up in a tight hug. "So yes, if you're leaving, I am too. If you're sure you don't mind driving, we can go home."

"Thank you."

"You're welcome, but please, calm down. I don't want you driving angry." The last thing they needed was another accident.

"Okay."

They made their way back to Tally's cabin at a much slower pace. Tally would be taking a pain pill at the first opportunity. The drive home wouldn't be pleasant, but she would suffer gladly if it meant helping Caitlyn through this.

CHAPTER FOURTEEN

They had been on the road for the last two hours and were into the final stretch of motorway before pulling off and heading to Tally's flat. The next hour couldn't be over with soon enough for Tally. Although her leg had gotten a lot better in the last couple of weeks, sitting still in Caitlyn's car was causing it to cramp every few minutes. Caitlyn had been silent on the drive, save for occasionally asking for directions. Tally wanted to ask how she was feeling, if she wanted to talk, but knew Caitlyn wouldn't want to. She hoped the time spent driving had allowed Caitlyn to process everything and see things more clearly.

"I'm sorry," Caitlyn murmured a few minutes later.

"What for?" Tally straightened her leg and flexed her toes, trying to stretch out her thigh.

"You're in pain, and it's my fault. I should have just gone to a hotel or something."

Tally relaxed her leg and sat up straighter. "You know, I could say I'm fine and don't worry about it, but I'd be lying. You're right. I am in pain, but we'll be home soon and I can stretch out in bed. This isn't your fault."

Caitlyn gripped the wheel tighter. "Tally, I'm sorry," she repeated with more force in her voice.

Tally reached over and squeezed Caitlyn's thigh. "Thank you. I'll be fine." Caitlyn nodded but didn't speak. *At least she's talking. Now might be a good time to ask how she is.* "Are you okay?"

Caitlyn shrugged. "She lied all this time. I get she didn't mean it to happen, but she didn't need to hide the truth from me. I would have understood."

"Cait, you have to think about her frame of mind at the time. She had just lost Karl and was on the verge of losing you too. She obviously wasn't thinking clearly."

"But she could have told me later, when I was better."

"The trouble with lies is, the longer they go on, the harder it is to tell the truth."

Caitlyn stiffened, and the car sped up slightly.

"I'm not taking her side. I'm just trying to see her point of view."

Caitlyn sighed and slowed her speed. "I thought things were black and white with police officers."

Tally smiled. "Not for all of us. No matter what situation I'm in, I always try and see all sides."

"Is that what you did with the guy who ran you over?"

Tally sucked in a breath. She had not expected that question.

"Shit, sorry. I shouldn't have asked that."

"No, it's okay." Tally shifted in the seat to find a more comfortable position and gave Caitlyn's question some thought. "When it happened, I was angry with him. He could have killed me. But being an officer comes with a certain level of risk. Of course, you never expect to be injured on the job, but it's a chance we take. During the investigation, Ryan found out that the guy was on drugs and alcohol. His wife also. She had been the one to attack him with the knife, and he had managed to get it off her seconds before we arrived. When he saw us, he panicked and just wanted to get away. Being hopped up on stuff, he wasn't thinking clearly. He'll still go down for his actions, but what he did wasn't intentional."

"So you forgave him?"

Tally shook her head, even though Caitlyn couldn't see her in the dark of the car. "I think I have to if I'm ever going to move on with my life. I'm still angry. I probably always will be, but I can't let it ruin my future. He made a terrible mistake, one he's paying for."

"So are you."

"Yes, but I'll heal and move on."

"You're stronger than I could ever be."

"You're strong, Cait. You've come through so much yourself. Don't let this thing with Selma ruin how far you've come."

"I guess, but I need time."

"Perfectly normal. Take the next exit."

Twenty minutes later, Caitlyn parked the car in Tally's designated spot. Tally glanced through the windshield to the second floor of her building. A light was on in her apartment. She frowned. Only her mother had a key, and she was still on the cruise as far as Tally knew.

"What's wrong?" Caitlyn asked.

"The light is on. I know I turned everything off, as I wouldn't be home for a couple of months. Someone is in there."

"Should we call the police?"

Tally looked over at Caitlyn and grinned. "I *am* the police."

"You know what I mean. What if it's an intruder?"

"Let's go find out." Before Caitlyn could stop her, Tally got out of the car. Her leg throbbed in time with her pulse but settled after a few seconds. She retrieved her crutch and made her way to the main door, fishing her keys out of her pocket as she did so. Caitlyn joined her just as she released the door.

"This isn't a good idea," Caitlyn said.

"It's probably Jimmy." Tally wasn't certain of that but could tell it eased some of Caitlyn's tension. They gradually made their way up the stairs, going slowly because of Tally's injury. They made it to her door. Tally turned the handle, surprised it was unlocked. Tally took a breath, then pushed the door wide. Her crutch clattered to the floor when she saw who was sprawled out on her couch. "What the hell are you doing here?" she shouted.

Bleary blue eyes popped open, wide with fright, then relaxed. "There you are. I've been wondering when you'd get home."

"Who is it, Tally?" Caitlyn asked, peering over Tally's shoulder.

"Annabelle."

"Oh."

Annabelle's gaze flicked over to Caitlyn, her lips pulled into a frown. "And who are you?"

Caitlyn stepped to the side of Tally and took her hand. Annabelle squinted at the gesture. "I'm Caitlyn. Tally's girlfriend."

"That didn't take you long, did it?" she asked Tally.

Tally had the urge to stomp over to Annabelle, grab her by the arm, and throw her out. It was only Caitlyn's hand in hers that prevented her from doing so. *How dare she come back here and try to make me feel bad for moving on.* "What I get up to is of no concern of yours. Not anymore." She let go of Caitlyn and picked up the crutch. She took a few steps forward. "I'll ask again. What are you doing here?"

Annabelle looked away for a moment, wringing her hands together. "I was wrong to leave. I tried calling you, but you must have blocked me or something, because I couldn't get through. I tried calling your mum and Jimmy and Ryan, but no one would talk to me."

"There's a very good reason for that."

Annabelle reached out, but Tally took a step back. Annabelle huffed. "Look, I know I messed up, but I was hoping we could talk." She glanced at Caitlyn, who still stood by the door. "In private."

"I have nothing to say to you. You left. I moved on. I want you to leave."

"Please, Tally. You must understand. I couldn't cope with it. Your nightmares, the mood swings, having to wash you. It was all too much."

Tally's breathing increased, and her free hand balled into a fist. She didn't like the situation any more than Annabelle did. She hated being looked after. That was the main reason why she went to Leighton Lake. Annabelle hadn't talked to her about the way she was feeling. If she had, they might have been able to work things out. But she hadn't. She ran out on Tally in the middle of the night without a word.

"I get that. I really do. But you left me. You made sure I was zonked out on pain meds, packed all your things, and walked out. You don't get to come back now and ask for forgiveness."

"But I love you."

For a moment, Annabelle's tears tugged at Tally's heart. She couldn't help but think of the years they had spent together, the plans they had made. But like a bucket of cold water being tipped over her, she remembered the pain of waking that morning with Annabelle gone. With no explanation, she had just vanished from her life.

Then she thought of Caitlyn.

The way she felt for Caitlyn was so much more than she ever felt for Annabelle. There was no choice to make. She and Annabelle were over. Even if Caitlyn weren't in her life, she still wouldn't want Annabelle back. She straightened her spine and felt the strength she projected, as she stared at Annabelle. "I don't care. I'm in love with someone else, and you need to leave."

In an instant, Annabelle's tears dried up. Her frown turned to a scowl. "How can you say that. You barely know her."

"I don't owe you an explanation, but here you go anyway. It doesn't matter how long I've known Caitlyn. She's the one for me. I love her, and I know she loves me. So please, just get your stuff and go."

Annabelle didn't move for a minute. Finally, her shoulders dropped and she hastily packed up the rucksack she had next to the sofa. Without saying another word, she stormed past Tally and shoulder bumped Caitlyn on her way through the door, then slammed it behind her.

Silence filled the apartment.

Tally stood stock still, her heart beating rapidly. The last thing she had expected was to find Annabelle sleeping on her couch. She would have preferred an intruder. The pain in her leg finally made itself known, and she slumped onto the cushions. She lifted her leg and leaned back, closing her eyes. She felt Caitlyn's fingers brush through her hair and soft lips touch her forehead.

"Are you okay?" Caitlyn asked.

Tally nodded imperceptibly. She opened her eyes. "I'm sorry you had to see that."

"It's all right. I just want to make sure you're okay."

"I'm fine. Are you?"

Caitlyn grinned. "I guess that makes us even."

Tally raised her brows in question.

"We both have crazy exes."

Tally laughed loudly, glad the tension had been broken. She turned serious. "I meant what I said. I love you." As adults, they may have only known each other a short while, but Tally knew her love for Caitlyn was real.

"I love you, too." Caitlyn dipped her head and kissed Tally on the mouth. The caress lacked the passion of some of their steamier kisses but was much more thrilling. The tender touch of Caitlyn's lips punctuated her feelings for Tally, and Tally loved every second of it. After a few more moments, Tally pulled back. "It's still dark out. Do you mind if we go to bed for a while? I'm exhausted."

Caitlyn smiled. "I'll go get our things from the car. You settle in bed. I'll be there in a moment."

Caitlyn began to rise, but Tally tugged on her hand. "I want to make love to you, but I don't think I can tonight."

"It's okay. We've got time. You're worth the wait."

Tally watched Caitlyn grab the keys and head out of the apartment. She laid still for another few moments, before finally rising and heading to the bathroom then the bedroom. She didn't switch on the light. She knew the path to her bed by rote. She didn't know how long Annabelle had been there, but the duvet didn't smell like her. Grateful, Tally crawled into bed and stretched out her leg. She began to drift off and only barely felt Caitlyn crawling in beside her a few minutes later.

†

Caitlyn rolled over and opened her eyes, expecting to find Tally curled up next to her. Sunlight streamed through the open blinds onto the empty bed. Caitlyn got a good look at Tally's bedroom. *The one she shared with Annabelle.* After all the drama with Selma and the long drive, finding Tally's ex on the sofa had been the last straw of a very bad day. Despite Tally saying they were over, Caitlyn couldn't help but worry Tally might still hold a flame for Annabelle. They hadn't been broken up long, and with Annabelle now wanting Tally back, Caitlyn was scared she might end up losing the one person she trusted wholeheartedly.

Tally's bedroom was practically bare. No pictures hung on the walls. The dresser and wardrobe were white and clean, with no evidence of Tally's personality. It looked sterile. *That could be her police background. Everything in order, in its place.* Caitlyn tossed the duvet aside and went in search of

Tally. She found her sitting at the dining table, talking on the phone. Caitlyn stayed by the bedroom door, listening.

"I promise, Selma… No, honestly, I'm fine… Yes, I will… Thank you." Tally hung up and turned in her chair, a welcoming smile on her lips when she saw Caitlyn. "Hey, good morning."

Caitlyn pushed off the door frame and walked over, confused over how she felt about Tally talking to her mother. She leaned down and kissed Tally quickly. "Morning." She sat down in the chair next to her. "My mum?"

Tally nodded. "I wanted to let her know we arrived safely." Tally reached out and took Caitlyn's hand. "She's worried about you."

Caitlyn looked away, her confusion escalating. Her head was all mixed up with lies and memories. If it weren't for Tally's compassion and understanding, she would be a nervous wreck and no doubt be swimming laps in the lake. She gazed back at Tally. "I'm not mad about them falling in love. It's the lies she told after. I understand what you said last night about lies getting out of control, but she could have talked to me." She shook her head. "I just can't deal with it all right now."

"It's okay. You can stay here as long as you need to."

"Will you talk to your mum about this?"

"Yeah, I think so. Not sure what I'll say, though." Tally ran her free hand through her hair. "This whole thing is crazy, but we'll get through this."

Caitlyn smiled. "I hope so." Her stomach rumbled, reminding her they hadn't eaten in the last twelve hours. "I don't suppose there is any food here?"

"There might be some bread in the freezer and maybe some fish fingers."

"That'll do nicely." Caitlyn stopped Tally from getting up. "Stay, I'll do it. Just tell me where everything is." After gathering what she needed, she lit the gas ring to cook the fish fingers. She placed the bread in the four-slot toaster and pressed the defrost button. As she began lightly frying, she glanced over her shoulder at Tally. "How are you this morning? How's the leg?"

"I'm good. I left a message at Emma's office to cancel the appointment today. She was supposed to have the results of the X-ray."

"Oh, God. I completely forgot." Caitlyn turned her back on the cooker, so she could see Tally better. "This was so selfish of me, dragging you back here."

Tally rose from the chair and approached Caitlyn. "It's fine. I'm a lot better than I was when I first arrived at the lake. Emma's exercises helped. If I don't improve in the next week or so, I can get an X-ray here."

"But still, I hate to think of something being wrong." Caitlyn was on the verge of tears. She should have left Tally down south to continue her therapy and found somewhere else to stay. It wasn't Tally's fault Selma had lied to her. But still, the thought of being away from Tally hurt her more than the lies. She didn't want to face the world alone. She wanted Tally. "We can go back."

"No."

"But—"

"No, no buts. We're here now. Let's just enjoy today and forget everything for a while." Tally cupped Caitlyn's cheek, her fingers soft against her skin. "My leg will be fine, and you and Selma will be all right. We don't need to worry about all that now." Tally kissed her lightly on the forehead. "The fish fingers are burning."

"Shit." Caitlyn spun around and moved the pan off the heat. She found some ketchup in the fridge and squirted it onto the bread. She added the fish fingers and plated the sandwiches. She joined Tally at the table. "What about Annabelle?"

Tally puffed out a breath of air before taking a bite of the sandwich. She swallowed and said, "What about her?"

Caitlyn picked up her half of the sandwich but didn't attempt to eat it just yet. She had a few questions she wanted to ask. Not wanting to be too intrusive, she hesitated. *Then again, we're supposed to be dating and in love. Don't I have the right to know?* "Do you think she'll be back?"

"Probably."

"What will you do?"

"I'll tell her to leave."

"Just like that?"

Tally nodded. "Yep. Just like that. I told you before; we had been drifting apart before my accident. Her leaving made me see we weren't truly in love." Tally reached across the table and took Caitlyn's hand. "I promise you; I have no feelings for her whatsoever."

Caitlyn desperately wanted to believe her, but her gut told her to be wary. *I guess time will tell.* Tally looked sincere enough. Her eyes were clear and focused, gazing directly at Caitlyn. Caitlyn had no reason not to believe her, so she nodded and changed the subject. "Okay. What do you want to do today?"

Tally looked away for a moment, chewing on another bite. "I could give Ryan a call, see if he's off work. I'd like him to meet you."

"I'd like that."

"Then that's what we shall do. And food shopping."

Caitlyn laughed, knowing Tally was making a dig at her overcooked fish fingers. "And maybe some wine."

"That'll be nice. I'm only occasionally taking my pain meds now. Provided my leg doesn't act up, I'd love a cosy night in with you."

"Sounds perfect."

†

Caitlyn stepped from the shower and wrapped an overly large white towel around herself. The hot water had done wonders to release the last of the tension from her body. Her mind was clear, and she could now see things from Selma's point of view. She was still upset over everything, but she was willing to talk to Selma. She wasn't sure when she'd return home for that conversation. Tally had been unable to get in touch with Ryan, so they decided to go visit some of the places Tally loved in her hometown. Caitlyn was more than happy to stay north for as long as Tally wanted. Yes, Caitlyn wanted to talk to her mother, but that could wait. She didn't know what was going to happen between herself and Tally when she went home. Would Tally want to come back with her? *Tally has her own life here.* For so many years, Caitlyn had been lost, adrift in her thoughts and feelings, confused about so many things. Being with Tally was the perfect cure for her self-anathema. With Tally, Caitlyn felt nothing but happiness, despite the few issues they both had along the way. The thought of going home and leaving Tally made her heart ache.

She entered the bedroom to get ready for their day trip. She had just started to lower the towel when Tally walked in. She felt Tally's gaze move over her semi-naked state, then settle on her face. Caitlyn watched Tally's chest rising and falling rapidly and saw her hands tightening into fists.

"Are you okay?" Caitlyn's own breathing increasing. It was obvious Tally was holding herself back from reaching out to her. Caitlyn wished she wouldn't. She wanted nothing more than to have Tally make love to her. She was tempted to drop the towel and see what Tally would do.

Tally's tongue peeked out and wet her lips. "I thought you were still in the bathroom." She glanced at the door. "I'll leave you to get changed." Tally took a step away.

"Don't go."

Tally turned around to face Caitlyn. "You know what will happen if I stay."

"Yes."

"Now isn't the time."

"Why? What's stopping us? We both want this. We've been waiting for this for weeks." Caitlyn slowly approached Tally. Her knees felt like jelly. She grasped Tally's hand and brought it to her cheek. "I love you, and I want to make love with you."

Tally swallowed hard. Caitlyn felt the full focus of Tally's intense gaze. "Are you sure? I don't mind waiting."

Caitlyn didn't know why Tally was so hesitant. For a moment, she thought maybe Tally wasn't as attracted to her as she had said before. Or maybe seeing her ex again had stirred up old feelings. She concentrated on Tally, on the fingers trembling against her cheek and on Tally's breath coming in near gasps. Her pupils were dilated, and Caitlyn's own gaze bored deep. No, Tally wanted this as much as Caitlyn. "But I do." Caitlyn let go of the towel, allowing it to pool around her feet.

Tally's gaze drifted down her body. "You're so beautiful. I knew you would be." Tally gently traced Caitlyn's collarbones and over her shoulders. "All that swimming has made you strong."

Caitlyn closed her eyes, as goosebumps raised on skin heated from Tally's touch. "How's your leg?"

"It's fine." With lightning reflexes, Tally swooped Caitlyn up in her arms and carried her over to the bed. She laid her down gently. "You mean the world to me."

"Prove it."

Tally grinned and quickly shed her T-shirt and jeans, leaving her in only a black sports bra and underwear. She joined Caitlyn on the bed and kissed her. Caitlyn gripped Tally's shoulders and pulled her on top, their bodies fusing. Tally's skin was so hot. Caitlyn's hands roamed over Tally's muscled back. She hooked her fingers under the band of her bra and pulled it over Tally's head. She cupped Tally's breast and gently squeezed. Tally sucked in a breath, her eyes shutting tightly.

They resumed kissing.

Caitlyn pushed Tally off and onto her back. She wanted a chance to look at Tally properly. She wrenched her mouth away. With laboured breath, she scanned Tally's body. Caitlyn knew the lightly tanned skin was Tally's natural colour and not from the sun. She trailed her fingers over Tally's chest and circled each nipple, Tally's stomach clenched in response. Caitlyn's gaze moved lower. Her fingers stilled as she saw the area around Tally's pelvis and hip.

"Jesus, Tally." Caitlyn studied the mass of scar tissue around Tally's hip joint and a couple of long, straight scars that she assumed were from the surgery. One still-pink scar ran down the outside of Tally's thigh. Caitlyn's hand shook, as she lightly traced the marks. She shook her head, feeling sick at the pain Tally must have been in when the car hit.

"It's not pretty, is it?"

Caitlyn's gaze flicked up to Tally's eyes. "It doesn't matter. All that matters is that you survived. Don't forget I have my own scars." Caitlyn lifted her hair away from the back of her head. "I was lucky this is all I have of my accident." She let her hair go. "We've both been through a lot." She cupped Tally's cheek. "I don't care what they look like, I just care about you." Tally half smiled. Caitlyn lowered her head and captured her lips in a ferocious kiss. Tally began to writhe beneath her. Caitlyn continued the kiss, while her hand drifted under the waistband of Tally's underwear. She slipped her hand lower, and Tally's pelvis rose to meet her. "If your leg starts to hurt, tell me and I'll stop." She dipped her fingers into Tally slowly. Tally groaned.

"I don't care how much it hurts. Don't you dare stop."

Caitlyn covered Tally's body with her own, her fingers still inside. She was careful to keep her full weight off Tally, bracing herself with her free hand. She relished the feeling of Tally's nipples rubbing against her own. She felt herself grow wet. She lowered her hips, so her clit touched the back of her arm and rubbed herself in time to her thrusts into Tally. Tally gripped Caitlyn's shoulders and pulled her more firmly against herself. A few moments later, Tally stiffened, her walls clamping down on Caitlyn's fingers.

"Oh, God," Tally cried, as her orgasm took hold.

Caitlyn continued thrusting and rubbing, until she, too, climaxed. She collapsed onto Tally, both breathing erratically. After a minute or two, Caitlyn pulled her hand free and lifted her head so she could see Tally. Tally's eyes were screwed shut, but a smile danced on her lips. Caitlyn gently kissed her. "That was awesome."

Tally opened her eyes. "Yes, it—"

Caitlyn's phone blasted out the theme from *Star Trek.* "Well, that's a mood killer."

Tally's body shook with laughter. "You'd better get it."

Caitlyn frowned, but she dutifully rolled away from Tally and off the bed. She retrieved her mobile and answered without looking at the caller ID. "Hello."

"What the hell is going on?"

Caitlyn almost dropped the phone at hearing Emma's voice blaring down the line. "Why are you calling me?" She hadn't spoken to Emma since the night of the barbecue when Emma had kissed her. She should have known she wouldn't go away quietly.

"I received a message from Tally, informing me she no longer requires my services. I've just spoken to your mother. She told me you two have taken off for a few days. What's going on?"

"It's none of your business."

"It is my business when my client runs off with my girlfriend."

"Are you fucking kidding me?" Caitlyn looked at Tally, who was now sat up in bed, a frown marring her satiated features from a moment ago. "For one, I am not your girlfriend. I want nothing to do with you. And two, if Tally no longer wants to work with you, that's up to her."

"You're fucking each other, aren't you?"

"I'm hanging up now."

"Does Selma know? I bet she—"

Caitlyn cut the call and tossed her phone down. She sat on the edge of the bed, head in hands. She had just had the most incredible experience with Tally, and now it was tainted. Tally moved and wrapped her arms and legs around Caitlyn from behind.

"Did you get any of that?" Caitlyn asked quietly.

"It was pretty hard not to hear it the way she shouted down the phone." Tally kissed Caitlyn's shoulder. "Are you okay?"

"I'm fine. I just wish she'd leave me alone. No doubt she'll call my mum and tell her."

"Are you worried about your mum finding out about us?"

Caitlyn shook her head and clasped Tally's hands, entwining their fingers. "Not in the slightest." She tilted her head to get a better view of Tally. "I plan on being with you for a long time. Mum will find out eventually. It just would have been nice if I could have told her myself."

"I love you."

"Me too." Caitlyn wriggled away and pushed Tally onto her back. "I know we said we'd go sightseeing today, but I find myself wanting to stay in bed."

Tally reached for Caitlyn and tugged her down. "Now, that is a plan I can get behind."

Thoughts of Emma and Selma were pushed to the recesses of Caitlyn's mind, as they made love again and again. They still needed to make a plan of what the future would hold for them, but for now, all Caitlyn wanted was to taste every inch of Tally's body. The rest could wait.

CHAPTER FIFTEEN

"Are you okay?" Tally asked from her position on the couch.

Caitlyn stopped pacing, a wry smile on her lips. "Yeah, I'm just a little nervous."

Tally shook her head. "There's no reason to be. Ryan is a great guy. You'll like him." Tally had called Ryan a few days ago to tell him she was back and that Caitlyn had come home with her. He had been surprised, but Tally explained the gist of the reason for the sudden departure from the lake. He sympathised with Caitlyn. It was his suggestion to come over and meet her. Tally was nervous, also. Ryan was her best friend, and she desperately wanted him to like Caitlyn. She planned on being with Caitlyn for a long time and needed two of the most important people in her life to get along.

"I'm more worried about him liking me."

"Cait, he'll love you." Tally stood and approached her. She took Caitlyn's hands in her own. "And not just because I love you. You're amazing."

Caitlyn's smile was electric; the corners of her eyes crinkled, as her cheeks raised. "You're biased."

"Maybe, but it's true." Tally tilted her head and gently pressed her lips to Caitlyn. She was about to deepen the kiss when a knock came at the door. "He's here."

Caitlyn ran trembling fingers through her hair.

"Calm down, you'll be fine." Tally opened the door and broke into a grin as Ryan came into view. "Hey, Ry. It's awesome to see you."

"You, too, T. It's been ages." Ryan stood a good four inches taller than Tally and solidly built. His big, blue eyes and dimpled cheeks lent a boyish charm to his otherwise imposing figure. He stepped forward and engulfed Tally in a tight hug. She held on around his waist, as he spun her around. "You're still a bean pole."

Tally wasn't a small woman. She had muscles in the right places but would never match the size of Ryan, hence the nickname. He let her go and grinned. Tally matched his smile, pleased to finally be in his presence. She stepped aside and allowed him entry. "Come on in." He walked through and glanced around before settling his gaze on Caitlyn. "Ryan, this is Caitlyn. Cait, this is Ryan."

Caitlyn shook his hand, her head tilted way back to see his face. "Hello," she said, her voice not as strong as it usually was.

"Nice to meet you." Ryan looked over his shoulder a Tally. "You're right, T, she's a looker."

Tally cut her gaze to Caitlyn, whose face was bright red. "Ryan!"

"Well, she is." He shrugged, his dimples deepening as he waggled his brows at Tally. "So what's the plan for the night?"

"I thought we could order pizza and play cards."

"Are you sure that's wise? You never beat me."

"Yeah well, I have Caitlyn here as my good luck charm." Tally took Caitlyn's hand, a clear sign she would have her on her team. She never could beat Ryan. Much like her father, she sucked at winning bets.

"Sorry to disappoint you both," Caitlyn said, "but if anyone will win, it'll be me."

"Ooh, she's feisty. I like that."

They settled around the kitchen table, beers in hand, and Tally dealt the cards. For the next hour, they bickered and postured over the games, while catching up on idle things. So far, Ryan was winning, with Caitlyn a close second. Tally was down to just a few chips left. In a couple more hands, she would be out of the game.

"So, how long have you two known each other?" Caitlyn raised the pot by a hundred.

Tally threw her cards down. "Fold. It's been about six years now."

"Yep." Ryan matched the bet and grinned at his cards. "We met my first day after I transferred in. She hasn't been able to get rid of me since."

"Nor would I want to."

He narrowed his eyes at Tally. "That car must have hit you harder than I thought. I'm not used to you being so mushy."

"It's the truth. I don't know where I'd be if it wasn't for your friendship. I never thanked you properly for staying with me after it happened."

Ryan cleared his throat, his cheeks tinting pink. "You don't need to thank me. I'm just sorry I couldn't stay longer."

"Yeah, I'm sorry about Annabelle. You should have told me."

"I didn't want to get in the way. She seemed perfectly capable of looking after you."

Caitlyn snorted at the comment and raised the bet again. "Sorry."

"Caitlyn's angry for the way Annabelle left."

"I don't blame her. It was a shitty thing to do."

"It was, but it doesn't matter. I'm glad she left. It was part of the reason why I went to the lake. If not for that, I wouldn't have found Caitlyn."

"And that is the only reason I didn't beat the crap out of her when we found her here on our arrival."

"What?" Ryan folded and Caitlyn beamed, as she pulled the pot over to her side of the table.

Tally smiled at the delight in Caitlyn's gaze. Her competitive streak was cute. She was clearly determined to beat Ryan. "When we came back, Annabelle was asleep on the couch. She wanted to give us another chance."

"I assume you threw her out."

"Of course I did. Not only was I not interested in seeing her, but I'm also with Caitlyn. I wouldn't change that for the world." Someone knocked on the door and Tally stood. "Pizza's here."

†

Caitlyn stacked her winning chips, as Tally went to the door. By her count, she had just overtaken Ryan. She was surprised her luck was in. She had never been any good at cards, but on this night, she couldn't seem to lose.

"I can see how much Tally loves you," Ryan said.

Caitlyn glanced up from her chips.

"It's not my place to ask, but do you feel the same?"

"It's okay, you're her friend. I expect you to look out for her." Caitlyn quickly looked over to the door, seeing Tally still with the delivery person. They were in conversation, and Caitlyn assumed he had delivered there plenty of times before. "You don't need to worry. I'll never do anything to hurt her. I love her with everything in me." She met Ryan's direct gaze with strength, wanting him to believe she was serious.

"You do, don't you?"

"Yes."

Ryan nodded. "Good enough for me."

"What are you two chatting about?" Tally placed the pizza box in the middle of the table.

"Oh, I was just telling Caitlyn about the time you tried to arrest that pensioner for driving his scooter down a bus lane."

Caitlyn glared at Tally, not sure she'd heard right. "You did what?"

"I wasn't arresting him, not for that anyway." Tally retook her seat and flipped the box open. The smell of melted

181

cheese filled the air. "I calmly asked him to use the pavement, and he started swinging his walking stick at me."

"Oh, God."

"It was so funny," Ryan said, laughing. "Here we thought he was this little, wizened old man, but he came out like a bullfighter."

"It wasn't funny." Tally scowled at Ryan. "He gave me a black eye. Jackass here was too busy laughing to help me. I had no choice but to arrest him for assault."

"Once we got him in the police car and he calmed down, Tally let him go with a warning."

"I can't believe you got beat up by an OAP." Caitlyn burst out laughing, holding her stomach. The image in her mind was hilarious, and she could just imagine how pissed off Tally would have been at having him swing at her.

"Hey, he probably fought in the war." Tally pouted. "He may be old, but he damn well remembered his combat training."

The evening wore on, and soon Caitlyn was wrapped up in Tally in bed. She lazily stroked Tally's belly while thinking over the evening. They'd had a great night. Ryan was a lot of fun, and she could see why Tally was so fond of him. Caitlyn didn't succeed in beating Ryan at cards in the end, but he promised to come back another day and give her another chance.

Without meaning to, Caitlyn started laughing.

"Why are you giggling?"

"I just can't stop thinking about you being attacked by an OAP."

"It's funny now. Back then, it was a little scary."

Tally didn't join in on the laughter, and her quiet response alerted Caitlyn that maybe it wasn't as funny as it seemed. "You were right when you said the job comes with risks."

"Yeah, you never know what situations you're getting into."

"Do you miss it?"

Tally sighed. "I miss the thrill of the chase, but I don't miss the tense situations. I used to thrive on the adrenalin. I think I'm done with it, though, at least for a while. The thought of putting the uniform back on and facing up to another situation where I could get injured makes me feel sick."

Caitlyn lifted her head and gazed down at Tally. "What do you think you'll do?"

"I don't know. I have time to think about it. Right now, I just want to concentrate on getting better and being with you."

"Ryan misses you."

One side of Tally's mouth lifted, her eyes shining. "I miss him too. He's like a brother to me. Even if I don't go back to the police, Ryan will always be in my life."

"I can see why you love him. He's a lovely man."

"Yeah, but a pain in the ass sometimes."

"He was just teasing you. I'm sure you do the same to him."

"You're right, I do. There was this one time he chased a suspect over a field. He slipped in cow shit and stank for the rest of the shift, despite the shower he took. I called him Poo Pie for like two weeks straight."

"I bet he loved that."

"He didn't mind me teasing him, but when the rest of the team joined in, he got mightily pissed off."

"Poor Ryan." Caitlyn laughed, but then she glared at Tally. "I just realised something."

"What's that?"

"You like to torment people."

"No, I don't."

"Yeah, you do. First me and the mud pie, and now Ryan and the poo pie. How many other people have you made pies out of?"

Tally rolled them over so she was straddling Caitlyn. "That's my little secret, and you'll never get it out of me."

"Wanna bet?"

"Sure." Caitlyn bucked her hips a few times but couldn't dislodge Tally's bigger frame. Changing tactics, she ran her hands up Tally's sides to her breasts and pinched her nipples. Tally yelped. Caitlyn hadn't pinched hard, but it gave her the chance to wiggle free. She pounced on Tally, knocking her back. Straddling her, Caitlyn leaned over and kissed Tally roughly. Passion overtook the playing, and they made love well into the night.

CHAPTER SIXTEEN

Caitlyn and Tally had spent a lazy day in the flat. By early evening, Caitlyn was getting restless. Tally suggested they go for a hike and a picnic. Caitlyn was pleased with the idea, but after only twenty minutes of walking, Tally was struggling. She said she was okay to keep going, but Caitlyn could see the strain her hip was causing her.

Caitlyn dropped the hamper onto the grass along with the tartan blanket. She looked over at Tally, who was puffing heavily next to her. "Are you sure you're all right?"

"Yes, I'm fine." Tally gave her a wan smile. "I'm sorry, but I don't think I can go any farther."

Caitlyn lightly touched Tally's forearm. "This is great. The view is amazing." They had made their way through the tree line and up a shallow grassy hill, not far from where

Tally lived. Caitlyn gazed across the expanse of fields toward the village. She drew a deep breath into her lungs, delighted to finally get some proper fresh air.

"Once I'm fully healed, we'll be able to go on proper hikes."

"That'll be good." Caitlyn turned back around and helped Tally unpack the kite they had bought from a local store on the way to their hike. "I loved exploring when I was travelling. I'd be gone all day, sometimes."

"Where did you go?"

"Everywhere. Greece, Spain, the Philippines, Canada."

"Wow."

Tally inserted the rods into the fabric, while Caitlyn tied on the set of strings.

"Where was your favourite place?"

"Oh, that's hard to choose. Probably Alaska. I did a four-week adventure trip, kayaking down the rivers and climbing mountains." She had so many different experiences in the four years she'd travelled the globe, but Alaska would always hold a special place in her heart.

"You just love the cold, don't you?"

"Yeah, as long as there is always a way to warm up afterward." She blushed, thinking Tally knew just how to get her hot.

"Do you think you're done with travelling, or are there more places you want to visit?"

"I'm done for now. Leighton Lake is all I need at the moment, but that may change." Caitlyn glanced up at Tally. As much as she loved Devon and the lake, Tally was becoming the most important thing in her life. She dreaded the day she would leave her to go back home.

"You miss being there, don't you?" Tally tied the tail to the main body of the kite, then checked everything was secure.

"Yeah. Although it's been just over a week, I feel like part of me is missing."

"Have you called Selma at all?"

Caitlyn shook her head. "No."

"She'll be worried."

"I know." She'd texted her mother the other day, to say everything was okay, but she didn't reply to Selma's questions about when she would be home. Caitlyn couldn't answer, as she didn't know. She still felt let down by her mother, for all the years of lying. With every passing day, her heart forgave a little bit more. She wasn't too old to admit she missed her mother. "Are you ready?"

"Sure." Tally held the handles of the strings, while Caitlyn took a few steps away with the kite. "Let her fly."

Caitlyn threw the kite in the air. It went up a few inches before twirling back to the grass and landing nose first.

"I said fly, not crash and burn."

"Hey!" Caitlyn picked up the kite, pouting. "You're the one with the controls."

"You're not big enough to get it up in the air."

"You do it then."

"Fine." They traded places. "Here you go." Tally tossed the kite, but the same thing happened.

Caitlyn laughed at the frown Tally wore. "See? It's not easy, is it?"

"Give me a second." Tally tried again. This time, the wind caught the kite. "There, it's up. Pull, pull, pull."

Caitlyn ran backward, tugging on the strings, trying to get it to go higher. The handles pulled at her fingers, and she struggled to keep hold. "The wind is too strong."

"Don't let go."

Caitlyn tried her best to control the strings, but a huge gust of wind slammed into the kite and tore it from her hands.

"Caitlyn!"

The kite went high in the sky, dangling its strings below, and floated off into the distance. "I am not chasing after it."

"I can't believe you let it go."

"It was hurting my hands."

Tally took Caitlyn's hands and kissed her palms. "Now what?"

"Picnic?"

"Sure. We'll need to get the kite before we go."

"It's probably miles away by now." Caitlyn laid the blanket out and set the basket on top, hoping the wind wouldn't take their food off in the same direction as the kite.

"It's in the trees over there. I'll go get it while you spread out the food."

"No, I'll go." Caitlyn stood. "I don't want you straining your leg."

"Are you sure?"

"Yep. Don't eat all the cheese." She jogged down the hill and found the kite in some branches. After a few jumps, she managed to snag the tail. She pulled the kite free of the tree limbs and went back to Tally. "It's a bit tangled, but we could probably try again."

"I think that's enough kite flying for the day." Tally grinned. "The sun will be setting soon. Let's watch that instead."

"Yeah, that's probably safer."

They ate in silence, while the sun began its descent. Once the salad and sandwiches had been devoured, Caitlyn settled in between Tally's outstretched legs, content in Tally's embrace.

"Are you warm enough?" Tally asked, her breath tickling Caitlyn's ear.

"I'm okay." She snuggled in further and watched as the sun dipped below the horizon. She never wanted to move. "It really is beautiful here." Her whisper was carried away on the wind.

"Not as beautiful as gazing out over the lake."

"No, but a close second. You're beautiful too."

Tally kissed the side of her neck, then settled her chin on Caitlyn's shoulder.

"I can't believe I found you," Caitlyn said. "I thought my life was fulfilled. I had my health, the lake, and Mum. I didn't think I needed anything more. When you showed up, everything changed. I can truly say I am the happiest I've ever been. You've made me complete, Tally."

"I feel the same. I don't want this to ever end. I love you, and I don't want to let you go."

Tally's voice was thick with emotion, and Caitlyn knew she was thinking of their impending separation. "I have to go home sometime, Tally."

"But not today or tomorrow?"

"No, but soon."

Despite the beautiful vista in front of them, a melancholy settled around them. Caitlyn's time there was ending. Caitlyn tried to block the sadness out from her heart, but it remained tucked away in the centre, causing a deep ache in her chest.

CHAPTER SEVENTEEN

Caitlyn sipped her coffee, surreptitiously glancing at Tally, who was nestled on the opposite end of the sofa. They had stayed in bed late again, taking the time to wake up slowly and enjoy a few lazy hours touching and kissing. There was no doubt in Caitlyn's mind that Tally was the love of her life. That didn't change the fact it was time Caitlyn went home. She'd spoken to Selma only once since they arrived, and it was clear her mum was missing her. Caitlyn missed her too. Despite the rift that now stretched between them, Caitlyn knew in her heart it would soon disappear if she just went home and talked things through. Her decision to return hadn't been an easy one. She wanted to stay with Tally. However, Leighton Lake was her home, and one she wanted to get back to.

She sighed, as she put her mug on the coffee table and shifted to face Tally fully. Tally raised her brows in question. "These past two weeks here have been the best of my life," Caitlyn murmured.

Tally grinned. "Yeah?"

Caitlyn nodded.

"For me, too." Tally's grin faded, as she pursed her lips. "You seem sad. What's wrong?"

"I was thinking that maybe it's time I went home. I need to clear the air with Mum and get back to work. I miss the lake."

"Sounds like a good idea."

Caitlyn nodded again, her pulse hammering. "I think so, however, I'm not sure what's going to happen between you and me."

"How do you mean?"

"Tally, we live miles apart." Caitlyn blew out a big breath, hating that they needed this conversation. *Why can't things be simple?* "I don't think a long-distance relationship would work. I love being with you, being in your arms every night. Making love. It's everything to me. I don't think I'd survive not being able to touch you every day."

Tally swallowed hard. "So what are you saying? Do you want to break up?" Caitlyn saw and heard Tally's panic.

"No, definitely not." Caitlyn reached over and captured Tally's hand. Her skin was cool to the touch. "That's the last thing I want."

"Then what are we going to do? I can't see you wanting to leave the lake."

"If I had to choose between you and the lake, you would win every time. But you're right, I don't want to leave there." That was confusing, even to her own ears. *How can I say she'd win and then say I don't want to leave home in the same breath? Could I really give up the lake? It's just a body of water, nothing special about it.* But the lake was special to Caitlyn. The water had been her only saviour in the years since her accident. *Until Tally.*

"I guess I could move down there with you. I'm not sure I want to go back to the police anyway, and I can visit my family any time I want."

"I can't ask you to do that, Tally. Your whole life is here."

"Cait, this is just a building to me. It stopped being a home months ago. All I see here now are shadows of Annabelle, and I don't want to live like that. I want to be anywhere you are. To be honest, being at the cabin was the most peaceful and relaxed I think I've ever been. It has this calming presence that settles something in me. It's almost magical."

"I feel that way too. I wasn't thrilled when Mum first bought the property, but after being there for only a few days, I fell in love with the place."

Tally looked wistful for a moment. "Perhaps…maybe, we could live in one of the cabins, or build our own. Obviously, if Selma doesn't mind."

"That sounds wonderful." That would be Caitlyn's choice. Living by the lake with Tally by her side would be a dream come true. However, Caitlyn knew it wasn't the right thing to do after seeing each other for only a few weeks. "Tally, are we moving too fast with it all? We've known each other for less than two months. You can't uproot your life after that short amount of time."

"So what do you suggest? I know I love you, and that isn't going to change."

"Maybe it's best if I go home, and we try long distance." Caitlyn shrugged. "If we're still together in a few months, maybe then we can think about you moving down."

"I'm not going to change my mind, Cait. I love you."

"And I love you, but for now, I think this is what we need to do."

Tally gazed at her for a long moment, biting her lip. Finally, she nodded her assent. "Okay. I'm going to miss you."

"Me too. While we're apart, you should concentrate on healing. I want you fit and healthy, so I can finally get you in the lake." Caitlyn smiled, but inside she was breaking.

"I'll get better, but you still won't get me in the lake."

"We'll see."

"We will still see each other though, won't we?"

"Yes. I'll come whenever I can, and we can Skype every day." Caitlyn cupped Tally's cheek, tears filling her eyes. "This isn't the end, Tally, just a new chapter."

"Promise?"

Caitlyn nodded. "I promise." Caitlyn leaned forward and pressed her lips to Tally's. She savoured the feel and taste of them, hoping against hope it wouldn't be the last time. She pulled back and rose from the sofa. "I'm going to pack my things." Now the decision had been made, she needed to leave before her resolve weakened and she changed her mind.

A half hour later, they were stood by Caitlyn's car, arms wrapped around each other, Caitlyn's head on Tally's chest.

"Call me when you get home," Tally whispered, her voice breaking.

"I will."

"I hope all goes well with Selma."

"I'm sure it will. It might take me a little while to adjust to her secrets, but I'm willing to move on from it all."

"Good." Tally stepped back and kissed Caitlyn quickly. "I'll speak to you later, then."

"Yes. Goodbye. I love you, Tally."

"I love you."

They continued to stare at each other for a few minutes, no words being spoken. They had said everything that needed to be said. Caitlyn, however, found it impossible to leave until she knew for certain Tally would be all right. She gazed at Tally, silently imploring her to say it was okay to go.

"Tally, if I don't leave now, I never will."

A tear slipped from Tally's eye. "It's hard to let you go."

"I'll call you in a few hours." Caitlyn wiped away Tally's tear, her own threatening to fall. *This is harder than I imagined. How is it you've got me so completely in love with you in such a short space of time?* It didn't matter how. Tally would forever be Caitlyn's soulmate.

Tally nodded and stepped farther back. "Okay, go now, before I drag you back upstairs."

Caitlyn smiled sadly and climbed into the driver's seat. Without looking at Tally, she started the car and pulled away. The drive home would be long and full of sadness. She couldn't help but think this was a mistake. *I should have agreed to let her come home with me. But what if it doesn't work out? That's not fair on her. No, you're doing the right thing. It'll just take some adjustment for you both.* She hoped that was true.

†

Caitlyn pulled up to the main house, her stomach clenching. The sadness of leaving Tally was now replaced with anxiety at seeing her mum again. She shot off a quick text to Tally to say she had arrived safely, then got out of the car. Lunchtime had passed, so she expected to find Selma in the kitchen clearing up. Steve and Fredrick ate lunch with Selma most days. Caitlyn walked around the outside of the house toward the back. As she glanced through one of the windows, she saw Selma standing at the sink washing dishes. Caitlyn climbed the steps and opened the door.

"Hi, Mum."

Selma looked up and dropped the plate she was holding back into the sink. "Caitlyn, you're home." Selma quickly wiped her hands on a tea towel and rushed over, enveloping Caitlyn in a tight hug. "God, I'm so sorry."

Caitlyn tightened her arms around Selma's waist, the familiar smell of her mum bringing a warm comfort to her shattered heart. She wanted to cry, but she held back the tears. She'd be Skyping Tally later. It wasn't like she was never going to see her again. That didn't stop her from missing her already. "It's okay. I've had time to think about things. I'm still upset you lied to me, but I understand you were in an emotional place and didn't mean for it to get out of hand."

Selma pulled back, the shame on her face wasn't hard to miss. She looked to the floor. "It was wrong of me, but once the lie came out, I couldn't seem to find the right time to put it right. After a while, I thought it didn't matter anymore. You were doing well, and life got back to normal." Selma glanced up. "Still, I should have told you."

"It's okay. Let's just move on from all this."

"Thank you." Selma took Caitlyn's hand and drew her to the dining table. They settled down next to each other, Selma still clutching Caitlyn's hand. "How is Tally coping with knowing about her mother and me?"

The mention of Tally brought a rush of heat to Caitlyn's cheeks. Memories of their time together flashed through her mind, and it took all her energy not to squirm in her seat. She ran her free hand through her hair. "She's fine with it, I think. She's going to talk to Dee when she's back from her cruise, but she's not going to mention it to her dad, I don't think."

"I'm pretty sure Herbert knew something was going on. Dee never really talked about it with me."

"How did you manage to go on, knowing you two loved each other but couldn't be together?"

Selma shrugged and her fingers twitched against Caitlyn's palm. "I don't know. It was a struggle at first. Dee was my soulmate. Eventually, days turned into weeks and then months. Before I knew it, years had passed and the hurt was no longer at the forefront of my mind."

Caitlyn wasn't sure she fully believed her. Anyone with eyes could see the love Selma had for Danielle shining through her gaze. Caitlyn thought of her own situation with Tally. The thought of going through life without her nearly brought her out in a cold sweat. Selma was much stronger than Caitlyn could ever be. Caitlyn had the urge to drive back to Nottingham. She doubted that would ever fade. "And you never wanted to find love with someone else?"

"Dee will always have my heart. Being with anyone else wouldn't compare."

"Yeah, I can understand that." Caitlyn looked away, as she remembered making love with Tally early that morning before the sun had come up. The memory brought about a shot of arousal, and she did squirm in her seat. *I never should have left. What have I done?* Although glad to be home, she was now coming to realise she had been hasty in her choice.

"Is that how you feel about Tallulah?" Selma asked.

Caitlyn blew out a breath. "Emma told you then."

"She did, but I already knew."

"How?" Caitlyn's brows pinched together.

"Caitlyn, since you came out of the hospital you were a loner. You travelled on your own and never made friends. I was shocked when you started dating Emma, but it was clear you weren't comfortable with her."

"Then why did you try to set us up again?"

"I just hated seeing you alone. I wanted you to have someone. When Tallulah came down, your whole demeanour changed. You weren't so in your own thoughts all the time, and you slept for longer. I figured it was your friendship with Tallulah that made the change. I knew, for certain, something was going on between you when I came up to ask you to help me find Houdini, the night you left."

"I didn't know he was missing."

"Yes. I came up to the cabin to ask for your assistance and saw you and Tallulah huddled together in front of the fire."

Caitlyn's cheeks burned, knowing her mother had caught them together. Not that they were trying to be secretive about their time together, but she was still embarrassed. "Why didn't you say anything?"

"I left you to your evening, found Houdini on my own, and went to bed. I figured you'd tell me when you were ready." Selma shrugged. "A few hours later you woke me up. We argued and you left. It was clear how much you two loved each other when Tallulah left with you, and the fact you've been with her for the last two weeks."

"And you're not mad?"

Selma smiled widely. "Of course not, dear. I love Tallulah. I couldn't ask for a better person for you."

"Is it strange we both fell for the Roberts girls?"

"No, they are hard to resist."

"Yes, they are. How do you think Dee will take it when she finds out?"

"I have no idea. I'm sure she'll be happy for you two. But if you're together for a long time, I'm not sure how Dee will feel being tied to me." Selma looked away. "We're still friends, but there is a distance there that I don't see shortening."

"Do you think she still loves you?"

Selma's eyes went wide, she looked mortified at the prospect. "I hope not."

"Why?"

"When you love someone, you want them to be happy. Dee chose Herbert, and I hate to think of her pining for me all these years and never truly being contented. All I have ever wanted was for Dee to be happy."

"Even though it breaks your heart?"

"I'm getting too long in the tooth to worry about my heart." Selma patted Caitlyn's arm. "I've got you, and I've got the lake. I don't need anything more." Her mum's smile was reassuring, but Caitlyn knew her well enough to realise she didn't truly believe her own words. Caitlyn didn't get a chance to question her further, as Selma said, "So, what about you and Tallulah? What are your plans for the future?"

"Long distance for now. We talked about her moving down here, maybe having a cabin of our own, but I think it's

way too soon for that. We haven't been together long."
Caitlyn's fingers drummed on the table, her restlessness
coming back for the first time in weeks. *I'm going to need a
good long swim.*

"Caitlyn, let me give you some advice. If you love each
other, grab onto one another and don't let go. Life is too
short to be miserable. If you move in together and it doesn't
work out, at least you tried and will have no regrets. You and
I both know how quickly things can change for the worse.
Don't waste a moment of the time you could have with each
other."

"I guess you're right. It's just such a big decision. She
knows I never want to leave here, so I'm basically asking her
to uproot her life for me."

"And you think she will begin to resent you for that?"

"Yes. How can I ask her to do that when I'm not willing
to do the same?"

"Did she ask you to move?"

Caitlyn shook her head. "No. She said she knows I love
this place too much. She loves it, too."

"Well, there you go. She obviously doesn't mind
moving."

"It's too soon." She shook her head again. "I think it best
we just carry on getting to know each other and see where we
are in a few months." *I'm lying to myself. I want her here,
now. I don't want to wait. Then what's stopping me?*

Fear.

"I wish you'd change your mind. Tallulah is one of the
good ones. You'd be a fool to hesitate."

"Then I guess I'm a fool." In her heart of hearts, Caitlyn
knew what she wanted, but she was too chicken to ask for it.
Asking someone to give up their life for you wasn't fair. She

had no right to be so demanding. As she said, how could she ask Tally to do the one thing she couldn't do herself. *No, it's best to stick to the plan.* She wasn't happy about it, but that's what they needed to do.

For the rest of the day, Caitlyn helped Selma around the cabins and went for her swim. She kept herself busy until the early evening, when she would finally be able to call Tally. Seeing her on the screen wouldn't be enough, but she would have to get used to it.

CHAPTER EIGHTEEN

Tally set her laptop down on the kitchen table and booted it up. Caitlyn was due to Skype her in ten minutes, and she wanted to be set up ready so she didn't miss the call. They had video called every night since Caitlyn left and sometimes texted each other into the early hours. Tally missed her so much. Being out of work lent her plenty of time to think. Missing Caitlyn might not be so bad if she had something to fill her time. All she was doing was her exercises and catching up with Ryan and Jimmy. That still left plenty of time for her thoughts to wander to Caitlyn. Tally was desperate to touch her again. Caitlyn had left only a few days ago. To Tally, that was a lifetime. She couldn't understand why Caitlyn was refusing her offer to move down with her, even on a trial basis. A three-hour drive was nothing in the grand scheme of things. She would still be able to see her family and friends as often as she wanted.

The laptop finished loading, Tally stared at the screen, waiting for the call to come in. She flinched at the annoying Skype ringtone. She clicked the answer button, and Caitlyn's pretty face filled the screen. Her hair was damp, and Tally knew she had likely just come from the lake. She looked tired, but also pleased to see Tally. Tally waved, feeling like a dork. "Hi, Cait. How are you?"

"I'm okay. Missing you like crazy though."

"Me too. It's only been a week, and I'm already pulling my hair out."

"I know the feeling. The only positive is I'm in the lake twice a day." Caitlyn ruffled her hair. "It used to help quell my thoughts, now it quells my sexual frustration."

Tally grinned. "It's good to know I'm not the only one suffering." Caitlyn's cheeks flushed, and Tally knew Caitlyn was remembering the phone sex they'd had two nights ago. The unique experience had started a little uncomfortably, but they both soon got into the mood. It didn't compare to the real thing, but it was a close second.

"How's your leg?"

"About the same. I'm getting stronger and no longer need the pain meds or crutches. I really think it was my lack of motivation that stopped me from getting better quicker. It cramps occasionally, if I overdo it, but nothing like how it used to be."

"That's amazing. You'll be back to your old self soon enough."

"Yeah, hopefully. Mum and Dad are back from their holiday next week. It'll be good to show them how much better I am."

Caitlyn glanced away for a second. "Will you tell them about us?"

"Of course. You're the best thing to ever happen to me. I can't wait to see you."

"Things are crazy here right now, getting ready for the summer season. We're pretty much booked solid already. I'm not sure when I'll be able to come up."

"What if I come down to see you?"

"I don't think you should be driving just yet, not until your leg stops seizing up. It'll be too dangerous. Maybe in a few weeks."

Tally had spent enough time with Caitlyn to recognise when she was being evasive. Tally's heart sank. She wondered if Caitlyn was trying to fob her off, if maybe she didn't want to be with her anymore. She looked at Caitlyn carefully. Underneath the pretence of worrying about Tally's leg, Tally noticed her eyes moistening, the slight tremor of her lower lip. Caitlyn was trying to be strong for them both. Tally could only assume it was to protect them from heartbreak. *Not that this separation is much better.*

"I don't think I can wait that long, Cait. Nothing feels right without you with me." Tears slipped from Caitlyn's eyes. Tally reached up and touched the screen in a desperate attempt to feel her. "Please, don't cry."

"I'm sorry." Caitlyn swiped the tears away with the back of her hand. "I just hate that we have to be apart like this."

"I know. I do too, but you said long distance was what you wanted."

"Yeah, but I didn't think I'd miss you this much."

"Then maybe we should rethink my moving down there. I can put the flat on the market and have an agent sell it for me."

"Tally, no. It's too soon."

"So, in which case we both have to be miserable for the foreseeable future."

"Please don't say that."

"It's true though. We both hate this. I don't understand why you're being so hesitant about me moving down there."

"I just don't want you to regret it."

"I could never regret being with you." A knock sounded on her front door. Tally glanced away from the screen. "Damn it, that's Jimmy. He's taking me to the pub for a drink and a few games of snooker." He wasn't due for another hour, which would have given Tally plenty of time to talk to Caitlyn. His eagerness to go out pissed her off.

"I'll let you go then. Have fun." Caitlyn's hand came into view for a second, then the screen went black. Caitlyn was gone.

"Cait, Cait, wait. Christ's sake." Tally slammed the lid shut and shot to her feet. She had been looking forward to talking about Caitlyn's day and telling her how much she loved her. Instead, the call had been a disaster. She stomped over to the door and pulled it open. "Hey, Jimbo."

"What's up with you?" Jimmy brushed past her and into the lounge. He flopped onto the couch and let out a sigh, as if he had been on his feet all day. Which he probably had.

"I was just Skyping Caitlyn."

"Trouble in paradise?"

Tally had told Jimmy about their relationship the day after Caitlyn left. She hadn't told him sooner, as she wanted to enjoy their time before Caitlyn went back to Devon. He'd been full of questions about why she ended her time away sooner than expected, and eventually she told him. He was all for them getting together. Tally didn't mention the situation with Selma and Danielle, only that Caitlyn fought with her mother. Jimmy hadn't enquired any more about it.

"She's upset we can't be together, but still refuses to let me move down there."

Jimmy quirked an eyebrow. "Are you sure she wants to be with you?"

"Yes, she does. She just doesn't want me to regret leaving this place and you guys." Tally sat next to him and stretched out her legs, pleased when no pain was present.

"Well, all your family and friends are here. I can see her point. But it's not like you're moving to another country, just a few hours away."

"You don't need to convince me. If I had it my way, I'd be there tomorrow."

"Then what's stopping you?"

"What?"

"What's stopping you from packing up and leaving?"

Tally tilted her head and gave the question some thought. "Nothing, I guess, but Cait said—"

Jimmy clasped Tally's shoulder. "Tally, listen to me. You nearly died when you got hit with that car, and so did Caitlyn when she had her accident. You've both been given a second chance at life. Don't you think you should stop playing around and grab onto each other? You never know what's around the corner. If she's the one for you, then you should go get her."

"But what if I arrive and she sends me away?" That would be more painful than getting hit by that car.

"Then you come home and lick your wounds. You won't know unless you try."

†

"Hi, Mum." Tally pulled the front door open. "It's good to have you home." Danielle's eyes gleamed above a huge smile. Her normally pale skin was tanned a golden brown, no doubt from sunbathing on the deck of the ship. Danielle wasn't much for exploring new cultures, so had probably spent all her time on the boat. Tally hugged her tightly, pleased to see her for the first time in two months. "How was the cruise?"

"Oh, Tallulah, it was wonderful." Danielle's voice was wistful. She brushed past Tally and into the kitchen. "We did so many interesting things. I've brought your father's laptop to show you all the photos we took." She lifted her bag off her shoulder and pulled out the computer.

"Sounds great. Dad not with you?"

"No, I left him at home doing the laundry. He lost a bet while we were away, and the loser had to do the unpacking and washing."

"I suppose you cheated at whatever the bet was." Her parents played that game a lot when it came to doing chores neither one wanted to do. Tally could count on one hand the times her father won. He never did figure out how Danielle always found a way of winning.

"Of course." Danielle's grin was conspiratorial. "How are you doing? You seem to be walking around much better. To be honest, I thought you'd still be at the lake."

"Some things came up, and I came back early." Tally sat down at the table, bracing herself. Now wasn't the time to be bringing up what she had found out, but she didn't see a time when it would be right. Being in the police had taught her that getting the truth out as soon as possible was always the better option. Lies festered and made things worse.

"Oh? Everything all right with Selma?" Danielle sat next to her in the adjacent chair, her forehead creased.

"She's fine."

"That's good." Danielle opened the laptop and switched it on. "Did you get along okay with her and Caitlyn?"

"Yes. They both looked after me well."

"I knew they would. They're good people."

"I need to talk to you, Mum, about what happened down there."

Danielle glanced at her quickly. "Um, all right."

"I know Selma told you about Caitlyn and Karl's accident." Tally took a deep breath. It was now or never. "I also know why you didn't tell me."

"Tallulah—"

"Let me finish." Tally held her hand up, palm forward. "A lot of things happened down there, some good, some bad. I should start by telling you that Caitlyn and I became lovers, while I was there. We fell in love."

"Oh." Danielle blinked, but held her features as though aiming for stoic control. "Okay." The corners of her mouth twitched. After a moment, she broke out in a grin. "Caitlyn is a nice girl, from what I remember. I'm happy for you both."

"Thank you." *She's not exactly jumping for joy, but that's understandable. She's probably worried about what I know.* "While we were spending time together, Caitlyn revealed she thought Selma was hiding something about the car accident. I asked Ryan to do a little digging. We found out the accident didn't happen where Selma said it did." Danielle didn't look at her. She carried on tapping away at the keyboard. If it wasn't for her breathing rate increasing, Tally might have thought she hadn't heard her. She ploughed on. "That night, Caitlyn had a memory come forth. She remembered seeing you kiss Selma."

"That's absurd!" Danielle shot to her feet, her cheeks turning deep red. "What nonsense."

Tally didn't blame her for the outburst. She didn't react, just carried on calmly. "Mum, it's okay. Selma told us about her feelings for you."

Danielle squinted her eyes, her gaze full of fury. "She had no right. That was private between the two of us."

"She cares a lot about you. That's why she lied about the accident. She didn't want you getting hurt by it, or Dad finding out about the two of you."

"Selma and I have never been anything but friends."

Tally leaned forward and took her mum's hand in her own and tugged her back to her chair. "But you loved each other?"

Danielle looked at the table and nodded. "Yes, but I was married to your father and had no desire to change that." She looked back up at Tally, her eyes brimming with unshed tears. "I was confused back then, but I know I made the right decision. Your father is who I belong with."

Tally squeezed her hand. "You don't need to convince me, Mum. I've grown up watching you two together. I never once thought you weren't happy with each other."

Danielle let go and leaned back in her chair. Her gaze drifted to the back wall. "Back then, Selma and I were so close. She was always strong minded and selfless. She'd do anything for anyone." She glanced at Tally. "When she told me how she felt about me, I freaked out. We were best friends. In those days, being a lesbian wasn't talked about. I distanced myself from her, but our bond was too strong. I found I was falling for her. I couldn't not have her in my life.

But there was your dad." A few tears spilled over, but she didn't wipe them away. "He was so kind and loving. I couldn't hurt him in that way."

"So you and Selma agreed to part ways."

"Yes. Our yearly calls are our only connection now."

"You must miss her."

"Of course I do. She was the sweetest, most caring person I knew, aside from Herbert." She took a shuddering breath. "But it was for the best."

"And when the accident happened?"

"I went down to see her before it happened. I missed her so much. We parted ways, not on good terms, and I didn't hear from her for a couple of weeks. She called to say Karl had passed and Caitlyn was seriously ill. I told her I would come down and be with her, help her through it, but she said no. She said our feelings for each other were what had caused the accident and it would be best if we stopped contact altogether. She begged me not to tell anyone, that we had all suffered enough."

You're both still suffering. So is Caitlyn. How can love destroy so many lives? "Dad doesn't know?"

Danielle shook her head. "He knows. I told him about the accident a few weeks later. He didn't question why I didn't go and see my old friend."

"Do you think he knew about you two?"

"I think so, but he's never mentioned it. I suppose he didn't feel the need to because I was with him."

Tally shifted in her seat and ran her hand through her hair. "This is all so crazy. So many lies and hurt amongst you all."

"It hasn't been easy, but we've just got on with our lives."

"Do you still love her?"

"Ah, Tallulah." Danielle tilted her head, a sad smile on her lips. "That's a difficult question to answer."

"Why?"

"I'll always love Selma. She was a big part of my life. Still is, I suppose. We will never be friends like we used to be."

"Why not?"

"It's complicated. Feelings like that just don't go away. It's been forty years, and she's still in here." She tapped her chest above her heart. "However, it's your father I belong with. He's the best husband and friend to me. I don't regret choosing to be with him."

"Maybe you and Selma could try to be friends again. It seems like such a waste after everything you've been through."

"No, it wouldn't be fair to her."

"Shouldn't she get a say in that?" Tally leaned forward, her gaze penetrating as she stared at her mother. "I know she still cares for you. I think you both need to talk it out, clear the air."

"We still talk."

"Not about the big stuff. You owe it to yourselves to at least try."

Danielle frowned. "I'll think about it. Does Jimmy know about any of this?"

"No. It's not my place to tell him. If you don't want him to know, I'm happy to keep it between us."

"Thank you."

"You're welcome. I love you, Mum." Tally stood and kissed her mum on the cheek.

"I love you, too." Danielle cupped Tally's cheek, love shining from her eyes. "You've grown into a remarkable woman."

"Thanks."

"Right, before I bore you with photos of the holiday, tell me about how you fell in love with Caitlyn."

"Well, it started when she knocked me flat on my ass..."

For the next couple of hours, Tally filled Danielle in on everything that had happened at the lake. They also talked more about Selma and Danielle's friendship and how maybe it was time to patch things up. Tally knew the bond between them was still strong. It was such a waste to let any more time go by without fixing it. Even though Selma and Danielle couldn't be lovers, it didn't mean they couldn't be friends. Danielle had a hard time believing that. She didn't want to hurt Herbert, but Tally tried her best to convince her to at least try. *And then we can all put this mess behind us and get on with being happy in life.*

†

"Are you okay?" Tally asked, as she turned off the motorway and onto the road that would take them to Leighton Lake. It had taken her two weeks to talk Danielle around into visiting Selma. Herbert had been stoic but supportive, when Danielle said they would be going away for a little trip. It was as if he knew it was time it was all laid to rest. Giving Danielle a chance to get her friend back was the right thing to do. A few days later, Tally and Danielle were on the road. Tally hadn't told Caitlyn they were coming. Their nightly Skypes had dwindled, and Tally feared Caitlyn was pulling away from her. Caitlyn said she still loved her,

211

but there was always a distance in her eyes. It broke Tally's heart to see her returning to her introverted ways. In the three and a half weeks they had been apart, a lot had changed, but also hadn't. Tally still loved her with all her heart and was determined to not let Caitlyn pull away from her. Jimmy was right. It was time to grab onto life and not let go. If Caitlyn sent her away, then so be it. She would take the chance.

"I'm nervous." Danielle fidgeted in her seat, punctuating just how anxious she was.

"Everything will be fine."

"I still think we should have called ahead."

"They only would have tried to talk us out of it." Tally reached over and patted Danielle's thigh. "I promise, Mum, Selma will be pleased to see you."

"I doubt I'll recognise her. It's been over fourteen years since I saw her last."

"She hasn't changed. Maybe a little greyer, with a few extra wrinkles, but she still has that indomitable spirit. Try to relax."

"How can you be so calm? If Caitlyn is anything like her mother, she'll be pissed you didn't respect her wishes."

"Caitlyn won't be angry. The only reason she doesn't want me to move down here is she thinks I'll end up resenting her for leaving my family. Once she sees how serious I am about us, her doubts will disappear."

"If you say so."

"I do." Tally saw the sign for Leighton Lake and smiled to herself. In less than five minutes, they would arrive, and she'd finally get to hold Caitlyn again. *Hopefully.* She wasn't a hundred percent sure Caitlyn wouldn't tell her to leave. The next sign came into view, and she turned down the gravel track. Her stomach tightened, but her heart felt light. *I'm home.* "We're here. Are you ready?"

"No."

Tally laughed, as she rolled to a stop a few yards away from the main house. Selma was out the front stacking logs by the front door, her back toward them.

"Oh my God, there she is."

Tally glanced at Danielle. "You're shaking."

"I can't help it."

"Come on." They stepped from the car, and Tally rounded the front. She took her mother's cold hand in her own and began walking.

Selma straightened and turned around. The colour drained from her face. "Dee?"

"Hello, Sel."

"What are you doing here?"

"Tallulah convinced me it was time to visit an old friend." Danielle cleared her throat. "How have you been?"

"Lonely." Selma's eyes filled, and tears tumbled down her cheeks.

"I'm sorry."

Selma shook her head. "Not your fault."

"Is Caitlyn around?" Tally asked. She wanted to give Selma and Danielle their privacy and was desperate to find Caitlyn.

"She's just gone to the lake," Selma replied, not taking her gaze off Danielle.

"Is Cabin Seven free?"

"Yes, the new arrivals won't be here for a couple of days."

"Is it okay if I steal Caitlyn for the evening?"

"Of course."

"Will you be okay, Mum?"

Danielle glanced at her quickly. "Yes. Selma and I have a lot of catching up to do."

"Okay. See you guys later."

Tally climbed back into the car and set off down the track toward Cabin Seven. She looked in the rearview mirror just in time to see Danielle and Selma in a tight embrace. Bringing her mother down to Devon had been a good idea. She just hoped Caitlyn would be as receptive as Selma.

CHAPTER NINETEEN

One, two, three, breathe.

One, two, three, breathe.

Caitlyn felt stronger than ever, as her arms pulled her through the water. The summer season was only a week away, and the lake was warming up. It was still cold, but not freezing like it was throughout winter and spring. She hadn't spoken to Tally in three days. Being in the lake was the only thing keeping her sane. After every phone call or video chat, Tally always brought up the subject of her moving down to the lake. Caitlyn always told her no. It wasn't that she didn't want Tally. She loved her completely. She just didn't want her to rush into a decision Caitlyn feared she'd regret. Three months was hardly enough time to know whether they would be together forever. Caitlyn didn't want Tally to uproot her life and have it all fall apart between them. In her heart of hearts, Caitlyn knew Tally was the one for her. She just needed Tally to be sure it was what she wanted too. *If she didn't mean it, she wouldn't keep asking you.* That thought had been buzzing around Caitlyn's head for days. Not once had Tally ever seemed hesitant in her wish to move closer to Caitlyn. *Then why don't I say yes? She loves you. You love her. What are you waiting for?*

One, two, three, breathe.

Caitlyn judged she had been swimming for about twenty minutes. It was time to check her position in the lake. On her next breath, she lifted her head to look around. She scanned the tree line, noting she wasn't far from the top of the lake. She did a few more strokes and checked again. Cabin Seven came into her line of sight. Her strokes stopped. She rubbed her eyes, not sure she was seeing correctly. *Tally?* Her form was unmistakable. Tally stood on the shoreline, dressed in shorts and a vest top. She waved at Caitlyn. Caitlyn still wasn't sure she was real. She kept her head above water, as she breaststroked the rest of the way across the lake. She kept her gaze fixed on Tally. Caitlyn feared she was dreaming and didn't want Tally to disappear. A few yards out from shore, Caitlyn's feet found the bottom of the lake and she stood. Slowly, she walked the rest of the way out of the lake. The cool breeze instantly chilled her skin. *She's here. She's actually here.*

Tally's smile was enigmatic, as she stared at Caitlyn.

"Tally? What are you doing here?"

"I got tired of long distance."

Caitlyn shook her head, droplets falling from her hair. "It's only been a few weeks."

"A few weeks too long. I never should have let you leave without me."

"Tally, we agreed it was for the best." Caitlyn looked away but continued to make her way up out of the lake. She stopped a couple of feet from Tally. She balled her hands into fists, stopping herself from reaching out.

"No, you agreed. I told you from the start I want to be with you. It doesn't matter to me where we are. As long as I'm with you, I'll be happy." Tally closed the distance between them.

"It's too soon."

"No, it's not."

"Tally—"

"Kiss me."

Caitlyn's gaze dropped to Tally's lips, their pink hue tempting her. She swallowed hard, desperate to feel Tally for the first time in weeks.

"I haven't seen you for nearly a month, Cait. Kiss me."

Caitlyn couldn't resist anymore. She took the last step toward Tally and grabbed her waist. She pulled her against her and crushed her lips to Tally's. Tally's tongue demanded entry into her mouth. Caitlyn obliged. At the first touch, Caitlyn's knees threatened to buckle. Tally tasted just as she remembered, and in that instant, Caitlyn couldn't remember why she ever suggested they stick to long distance. Her heart lifted for the first time since leaving Nottingham. Her jumbled thoughts left her. All she could feel was Tally. She broke the kiss, but she kept her arms around Tally. "I've missed you so much."

"Come inside, you're shivering."

Tally grasped Caitlyn's hand and led her up the steps into the cabin. Tally lifted the blanket off the back of the couch and wrapped it around Caitlyn's shoulders. Caitlyn pulled it tight around herself. She gazed up at Tally, still not quite believing she was there after all this time.

"Better?" Tally asked.

"Yeah." Caitlyn nodded and freed one of her hands. She cupped Tally's cheek, the warmth of her skin heating her more than any blanket could do. "I can't believe you're here."

"I'm never leaving again. I love you."

"I love you too. Take me to bed."

†

Caitlyn rolled away from Tally, gasping for breath. Her orgasm had been the most intense she had ever had. *I guess the weeks apart put me on edge more than I realised.* She wiped the sweat from her brow, as her breathing settled back down to its normal rhythm. She snuggled back into Tally's arms. All the swimming she had done in the last month didn't settle her as much as lying with Tally did. *I was an idiot to think I could do this without you.* She lifted her head from Tally's chest. "Does Mum know you're here?"

"Yes. She won't miss you though." Tally smiled up at her. "I brought Mum with me. I think they'll be busy repairing their friendship."

"Oh wow." *That's unexpected.* "What about your dad?"

Tally sifted Caitlyn's still damp hair through her fingers. "From what Mum said, he knows they loved each other, but he trusts Mum not to cheat on him."

Caitlyn screwed up her face. "I really don't need the mental picture of our parents doing it."

"Yeah, it is kinda gross." Tally let out a throaty chuckle. "I don't think Mum wants that anyway. She just wants her friend back."

"Mum feels the same." Caitlyn settled her head back down and released a contented sigh. "We talked a lot about what happened back then. She still loves Dee, but, more than anything, she wants her to be happy."

"Hopefully, this trip will patch up any old hurts, and they can finally be friends again."

"That'll be good. Especially as they'll be helping to plan the wedding."

Tally's fingers stilled. "Did you just propose?"

Did I? "Sort of. I'm not suggesting we get married now, but in the future?" She nodded slightly. "Yeah, that's what I want."

"Me too. I'm so happy you came into my life."

"I love you, Tally." Caitlyn kissed the bare skin just above Tally's breast. "Thank you for being brave enough to come back here."

"Nothing would keep me away from you." Tally tightened her arm around Caitlyn and started playing with her hair again. "We just need to live each day as it comes now. No more putting things off."

"Does that mean you'll no longer put off swimming with me in the lake?"

Tally laughed. "I guess not, but not tonight." She rolled over and braced herself above Caitlyn. "Tonight, I want to stay wrapped up in the warm, with you in my arms."

"Sounds perfect."

As they made love again, Caitlyn lost herself in the sensation of feeling fully loved. Tally was everything she ever wanted. The weeks they were apart were the worst of her life. She would always be thankful Tally took the leap and made the choice to go after what she wanted. Caitlyn was determined to never let her go. Images of them living in their cabin and swimming in the lake brought a smile to her lips. She drifted off to sleep some time later.

CHAPTER TWENTY

"There you are." Tally had found Caitlyn standing under a tree. "What are you doing up here?"

Caitlyn smiled at Tally, but her gaze never left the workers hammering and sawing logs in the patch of grass where she and Tally had their first picnic. "I couldn't stay away."

Today was the first day of the build of their new cabin. Although Caitlyn was supposed to be working, she couldn't resist coming up to watch. Tally had been living in the main house with Caitlyn for the last four months. Her leg was completely healed, and she'd been helping around the lake while she decided her next career move. Tally didn't want to go back to the police force, but she was no closer to figuring out her future employment. There was no hurry. She had no recurring bills to pay. The sale of her flat had been completed a couple of weeks ago, so she wasn't short on money. Her focus right now was contributing to the cost of the cabin.

Caitlyn's relationship with Selma had improved, and they were back to their old selves, laughing and joking and working well together. Everything had worked out right. She still didn't like Tally being so far away from her family and Ryan, but they all tried to get together when they could.

"Selma asked me to find you," Tally said. "Your favourite cow has wandered off again."

Caitlyn laughed. "I think he just prefers it over on our property."

"That may be so, but the guests are freaking out."

"They always do." Caitlyn grasped Tally's hand. "Watch with me for a minute?"

Tally nodded and wrapped her arms around Caitlyn from behind and rested her head on Caitlyn's shoulder. "In a few weeks, this will be our new home."

"I can't wait." Caitlyn turned in the circle of Tally's arms. "No regrets?"

"Not a one." Tally kissed the tip of Caitlyn's nose. "Mum is coming down next week with Jimmy and the kids. I can't wait to play on the lake with them."

In the months since Tally moved, Caitlyn had finally managed to get her swimming in the lake. After the first few times of screaming about the coldness of the water, Tally soon acclimatised. She seemed to love it now. She wasn't as good a swimmer as Caitlyn, but she still joined her most mornings for a lap around the lake.

"Is your father coming?"

Tally looked away for a moment. "No, I don't think so."

"Dee's friendship with Selma is causing problems, isn't it?" Tally rarely spoke about her parents' relationship, saying it wasn't her place. However, Caitlyn had an inkling it was because there were difficulties.

"He said he's fine with it, but every time Mum comes down here, he gets all sullen and moody. I suspect he thinks Mum still loves her."

"But they're just friends." In Danielle's few visits, Caitlyn had never noticed anything inappropriate between them. She could see the love Selma had for Danielle, but she never acted on those feelings. Caitlyn knew Selma was genuinely happy Danielle was with Herbert.

"We all know that, but Dad is going to need a little more time to adjust to their friendship, now it's renewed. He'll come around."

Caitlyn glanced over her shoulder at the workers. "I can't believe this will be our home soon."

"Me neither." Tally cupped Caitlyn's cheek. "I remember the day you literally knocked me off my feet. From that moment, you lodged yourself in my heart, and I never want to let you go." She lowered her hand and reached for something in her jeans pocket. "I was going to wait to do this later, but standing here with you, at the foot of our new home... I think it's the perfect time." Tally got down on one knee.

"What are you doing?" Caitlyn's left hand trembled, as Tally took it in her own. Her pulse thumped erratically, and she was sure she was going to faint.

"We've both been through a lot over the years. Together, I know we can face anything. I never want to be without you." Tally fumbled with the small velvet box, eventually getting it open. "Caitlyn Matthews, will you do me the honour of becoming my wife?"

Tears rolled down Caitlyn's cheeks. Her breath came in gasps, and she couldn't get the word out. She nodded instead. Tally beamed up at her and slipped the ring onto her finger.

"I love you so much, Cait."

Caitlyn grabbed Tally's T-shirt by the collar and pulled her up. She lunged forward and kissed her hard. Her life was complete. She may have lost her past, but there was no way she was going to lose her future. Tally was everything, and Caitlyn was determined to make her happy for the rest of their days. She pulled back and scanned the area around them. "I know we're supposed to find Houdini, but I have to have you now."

"Cabin Six is free, I think."

"That'll do." She grabbed Tally's hand and drew her through the trees and into their future.

The End

ABOUT SAMANTHA HICKS

Samantha currently lives in the south west of England with her best buddy, Finley, her springer spaniel. She spends her time writing, drawing, and getting out into nature. Family and friends are the most important things to her, and she finds her inspiration for her stories from those closest to her. Writing has become her greatest passion, and after years of trying to find her confidence, she's finally decided to make a career out of it. She hopes to be doing this for the rest of her life. Sam has a thirst for reading, preferring it to almost anything, and she hopes to one day settle down by the beach.

OTHER BOOKS FROM AFFINITY

The Others by Annette Mori

As a seer and brilliant scientist, Em convinces her wife, Lise, to prepare for the inevitable conclusion, after the chaos caused by foreign countries attacking the United States. Leaving behind a wake of destruction and a new world order, forcing them to navigate a frightening reality. After ten months in their cozy bomb shelter, they emerge to a world where the vegetation is surprisingly unaffected. Should they band together with other survivors, or try to make it on their own? There are others in this unknown world. On the first day outside of their shelter, they meet members of an alternate society. Are they friend or foe? Change is inevitable. But will they change in ways Em and Lise can live with, or will this altered world change them into something unrecognizable?

Three Mile Cache by Jen Silver

The story is set in Australia circa 1988. When archaeologist Carolyn Wells returns home to Sydney after several months away at a dig in Tunisia, she expects to be reunited with her lover, Detective Inspector Alex Graham. But she soon learns that Alex has been wounded in a hostage incident and is recuperating at a Royal Flying Doctor Service hospital at a place in the outback of New South Wales called Three Mile Cache. Carolyn decides to fly out there and surprise Alex with her arrival. Surprises abound when she gets there. One of the doctors treating Alex has a rather intimate interpretation of a bedside manner. There are mysterious goings-on at a local homestead and Alex's injuries haven't stopped her from probing into the lives of the locals, much to their annoyance. When Carolyn and Alex meet again, things don't quite work out as either of them would like. Can their relationship recover from the series of events in Three Mile Cache that threaten to keep them apart?

Sculpting Her Heart by Annette Mori
On the surface, it appears as if Zari Woods has achieved everything, she set out to accomplish fame, money, a supportive best friend, and loving parents. But to a person on the neurodiverse spectrum, a loving woman is elusive. When the right woman comes along she's already taken.

Soul on Fire by Ali Spooner
A perfect summer ends with danger on the Appalachian Trail for Whit, Mitch and Brad. Once safely home, the relationship between Eli and Whit continues to strengthen as the boys return home and they grow as a couple. Eli falls deeper in love with Whit and North Carolina as the trees

come alive with autumn color. The first Christmas at Cast Iron Farm is celebrated with Eli's family as a new chapter in all of their lives begins. Join the family for the third book in the Cast Iron Farm Series.

The Boss's Daughter by Samantha Hicks
Vivian Westfall, CFO of *Bridger Holdings*, meets her boss's estranged daughter, Lauren, when a disturbance at the company spring party piques her interest. Lauren is clearly drunk and making a fool of herself. To prevent embarrassment, Vivian forces Lauren away from the party. They have angry words, and things take an unexpected turn when Lauren kisses her. Months later Lauren pitches a proposal to her father to loan her the funds to start her own health club. Her father reluctantly agrees with a caveat; Vivian must go with her to Scotland to keep an eye on the money. It doesn't take long for the sparks to fly in all emotional directions. When Gregory Bridger finds out about their relationship, he does everything in his power to break them apart. Trust is at the heart of this love story, a fragile emotion that without it, things can and do fall apart.

The Ghost of East Texas by Ali Spooner
Agent Blair Cooper and her partner, psychic Tally Rainwater (Terminal Event), are back in a gripping new murder mystery investigation. When the serial killer Casper Caruso, known as The Ghost of East Texas, was sent to death row, Agent Blair Cooper was adamant that there were more victims of his killing spree. As his execution day approaches, Casper reaches out to Blair. If she agrees to a face-to-face meeting, he will give the whereabouts of 10 additional bodies left in his wake. Blair and Tally must piece together

the clues to bring closure for some of the victim's families. However, when you bargain with the devil, there is always a price to be paid.

Terminal Event by Ali Spooner
Tally Rainwater was born with the gift of second sight, something she never understood. A near-fatal accident, at age twelve, makes her visions clearer, but not the reason for them. As she matures, Lisa, a spirit, enters her visions to guide her in using her gift, but still not the reason why. Can Tally and Blair's budding romance survive the possibility? Read this intense murder mystery romance and find out.

The Star Child by Ali Spooner
Eli and Whit are enjoying their life together on the mountain when Whit is called into action for a secret mission at the Pentagon. While she is gone, the Cast Iron Farm comes to life, literally, when Eli discovers a mysterious cave that has a connection to Whit's past. Younger brother Brad joins the gang. When Whit returns, she plans an Appalachian Trail adventure with Brad and Mitch. Join Eli and family as their adventure at Cast Iron Farm continues.

My Dear Vet by JM Dragon
Ava Lawrence, a research veterinarian, is thrown in the deep end when her uncle asks her to cover his country practice while he has a vacation of a lifetime. How could she refuse? His team shouldn't be any different than the crew at her parents' practice, oh, was she so wrong. What she now has to work with is a sassy nurse, an obnoxious receptionist, and an animal whisperer, or so it seems. Ava finds herself embroiled in taking care of animals in the area and local

issues outside her experience, making her question her sanity. Throw in chickens, cats, dogs, and a donkey named Theo, along with various other animals. This turns out to be Ava's unexpected adventure with far reaching romantic benefits.

One Shot at Love by Annette Mori
Blair returns to her hometown after the death of her sister. Always an activist, she vows to use her voice to advocate for better gun control. She meets Maribel, an irresistible, sexy woman who proves to be an enigma to Blair. Maribel can't help approaching the weeping woman and learning the origin of Blair's grief, Maribel thinks she is the last person who should form a friendship with Blair. Ultimately, the allure is too much for Maribel, but how long can she keep her secret and continue to nurture their burgeoning feelings for one another. A committed left-wing social activist could never fall for the poster child of the NRA. Unless taking that one shot at love matters more than anything else.

The Mountain Whispers by Ali Spooner
Arriving home and discovering the betrayal by her best friend and lover, Eli Fortner leaves to run off her anger and hurt. A chance stop at a convenience store and the purchase of lottery tickets sends Eli's life into a whirlwind of change. Able to now pursue her dreams, Eli heads off to see what else fate has in store for her.

Whit Brewer, Eli's neighbor, is everything Eli never knew she needed and wanted. But can she let go of the betrayal long enough to let Whit in? Thirteen black cats, a baby goat, and Cruz, her furry best friend, join Eli on her adventure, new life, and the possibility of real love.

<u>Charlie</u> by Erin O'Reilly

At fourteen, Hannah Garvin met 'the one,' Charlene Gaines, and her life was never the same. They were inseparable and spent every moment they could together. One day, Charlie left without a word and again, Hannah's life took a dramatic change. Hannah vowed to never fall in love again. When she meets Mick, a new arrival to the small Texas panhandle town near her family's farm, her heart remembers what being in love was like, and yearns for more. Will Hannah let the memory of Charlie go so she can start a new life with Mick? Or will her heart betray her and hold on to her love for Charlie?

Affinity
Rainbow Publications

eBooks, Print, Free eBooks

Visit our website for more publications available online.

www.affinityrainbowpublications.com

Published by Affinity Rainbow Publications
A Division of Affinity eBook Press NZ LTD
Canterbury, New Zealand

Registered Company 2517228